I0690569

IRONY
and Somewhat Twisted Tales

First Edition

Published by the Nazca Plains Corporation
Las Vegas, Nevada
2014

ISBN: 978-1-61098-354-9
E-Book: 978-1-61098-355-6

Published by
The Nazca Plains Corporation®
Paradise Rd, Suite 141
Las Vegas, NV 89109-8000

PUBLISHER'S NOTE
Irony and Somewhat Twisted Tales is a work of fiction created wholly by Christopher Trevor's imagination. All characters are fictional and any resemblance to any persons living or deceased is purely by accident. No portion of this book reflects any real person or events.

Male Cover Photo, Anetta - Fotolia
Art Director, Blake Stephens

IRONY
and Somewhat Twisted Tales

First Edition

Christopher Trevor

Contents

The School Bully's Dad

Author: Christopher Trevor

It was around six thirty PM when Bill Titan, thirty-nine year old vice president for a leading bank stepped off the train and walked briskly to the block where he lived, a short distance from the train station. But instead of heading in the direction of his house where he lived with his wife and teenage son John, he strode across the street and a few houses down to where his son's classmate, Gene, lived, along with his parents, Frank and Eleanor Marone, Bill Titan's and his wife's neighbors. Feeling stressed from the long workday and all the office bullshit he'd had to put up with, this was the last thing he wanted to have to deal with, but it was his son's welfare that was on the line here, and he did not want John to be a victim at all.

At the door to Gene's parent's house Bill rang the bell twice, but no one responded. Thinking that perhaps the doorbell was broken Bill pulled the outer screen door open and rapped hard on the inner wooden door.

"Hello! Anybody home?" Bill called out. "Mr. Marone, Mrs. Marone? Anyone there?"

As he called out Bill rapped harder on the wooden door.

Then, from inside the house Bill heard a brusque sounding voice loudly saying, "AH jeez, now who can that be?"

Bill glanced quickly in the side window and saw Frank Marone, a burly construction worker, wedging himself up from a comfortable looking recliner and stomping for the door.

When the door was pulled open Bill took in the sight of his neighbor, still clad in his leftover construction clothes of scuffed up mustard colored construction boots, a white tee shirt that was ratty with sweat stains and an old looking pair of Wrangler jeans.

"Hey there, uh, good evening Mr. Marone, I'm uh, sorry to bother you at this time of day, as you can see I'm just getting home from work as well, and uh, well, I'm John Titan's dad, from up the street, Bill Titan," Bill began, trying to sound as pleasant as possible, the differences in the class of him and the burly construction worker instantly noted. "And you see, well, we have a little problem, well, actually our kids have the problem."

As Bill stood there yammering he also quickly noticed the way Gene's burly dad was taking in the sight of him, well-toned and fairly muscular in his thousand dollar navy blue suit.

"So what's the problem buddy?" Frank Marone asked Bill. "And yeah, I know your son John; he's friends with my boy Gene."

"Well, I got a call from the school principal and apparently they seem to be really going at it, actually the principal called me twice this week," Bill said. "He told me that he tried calling you and your wife as well, but no one answered the phone. When he told me who you were I told him that I lived nearby you and that I would come here myself and try to work this out. The incidents that the principal mentioned happened in our kids' gym class in their high school."

In response, Frank Marone grinned meanly, flexed his huge arms involuntarily it seemed and asked, "So what are you telling me Billy, that your boy can't take what my boy is dishing out on him?"

As the burly construction worker spoke Bill realized that he was already aware of what was happening between their sons, and he also detected a scent of hard-core male sweat emanating from the guy.

"Hey look, that isn't the point, the point is your kid needs to keep his own space," Bill replied, starting to feel angry now at this oaf's obvious ignorance.

"To put it plainly your boy is a bully and he's been harassing my kid."

"Look Billy," Frank began and Bill held up a hand, halting the man in his tirade.

"It's Bill, not Billy, thank you," Bill said and Frank grinned at him again.

"Okay, I was just trying to be friendly, *Bill*," Frank began again. "But look, our kids are just that, kids, and kids are going to have these things happen between them.

As he spoke this time, Frank reached out and took the bottom end of Bill's maroon colored tie in hand.

"Pretty tie Billy, I mean Bill, where'd you get this silk number huh?" Frank asked and brazenly stretched Bill's expensive tie out, the executive looking at the construction worker now in disbelief.

"What the fuck???" Bill reeled, looking stupidly down at his stretched out tie and the construction worker's paw-like grubby looking hand that was holding it. "Okay, yeah, they're kids, but they still need to learn and…"

"Say, you wanna come inside and talk about it Billy, I mean Bill?" Frank asked, now tugging a bit on Bill's tie. "We got the whole place to ourselves; the wife and kid are out."

"I'm uh, I'm not sure there is anything much to talk about," Bill said and then watched in disbelief as Frank bunched and wound his tie in his HUGE fist, proceeding to curl it around his wrist.

"Look, could you uh, let go of my tie and just ask Gene to keep his hands off my son John, and I'll uh, be on my way I guess," Bill stammered. "Like I said, there's really not all that much to talk about here…"

"Fuck that Billy, *there's plenty* to talk about," Frank grunted and yanked the executive forward by his tie, nearly hauling the guy out of his slip-on loafers.

"HEY…fuck…" Bill reeled as Frank then let go of his tie, and he stumbled and hobbled into the house, his arms flailing at his sides.

"Easy buddy, easy does it," Frank said and caught Bill by his suit jacket collar before he hit the floor.

As Bill righted himself Frank said, "Now I'll show you what a dad like YOU needs Billy," as he closed and locked the front door. With a feeling of disbelief coursing through his very being Bill then found himself being led to Frank's kitchen by his upper arm in the construction worker's meaty grip.

"Like I said, how about a beer while we talk huh Billy bud?" Frank asked, leading the executive toward the kitchen. "Say, can I call you that, Billy bud?"

In response Bill clenched his teeth, struggled away from the burly guy and straightened his tie. Instead of heading out the door of the house though, Bill Titan followed Frank to the kitchen, still straightening out his tie as he went.

"Sure, uh, I suppose a beer sounds reasonable," Bill said. "But calling me Billy bud does not sound reasonable," Bill said as he gathered himself and felt a bit better.

Grinning meanly, Frank held out a bottle of beer, but as Bill went to take it from him, Frank dropped it at the executive's loafer clad feet. The bottle shattered and the beer sprayed all over the executive's suit trousers and shoes and socks.

"HEY, oh holy shit!!!" Bill reeled now and stupidly hopped around in the mess. "Son of a bitch!! Man, are you fucking crazy? First you rumple my goddamned tie, and then you break a bottle of beer on me???"

As Bill hopped around in the mess of splattered beer, Frank, still grinning, stepped behind his houseguest, and tripped him to the floor, poor Frank landing on his ass, in the puddle of beer, with his feet pointing straight up in the air.

As he looked up at Frank Bill snarled, "You're nuts man, what a mistake I made coming here and trying to reason with you, I am out of here, Frankie bud…"

"Now, now Billy bud, you ain't leaving so soon, not when it's time for your homework," Frank said, reached down and grabbed Bill's navy blue dress socked ankles, tucked them tightly under his armpits, and then hoisted the executive up and laid out on his back as he faced forward. "You and me is gonna have some man to man fun first!"

As the burly construction worker hoisted Frank's ankles upwards and tighter under his armpits, the executive's loafers fell off.

"DAMN, let go of me you big overgrown oaf!!" Bill demanded as he wiggled his dress socked feet helplessly and then found himself being dragged across the kitchen floor, on his upper back.

"I have something that will teach you and YOUR SON to be real men," Frank said as he dragged the executive along and a look of sheer terror suddenly came over Bill's face, as he realized that he was suddenly helpless and in this nut-job's clutches.

Bill pounded the floor with the palms of his hands, reeled upwards for Frank to let go of him, as he was dragged back to the living room.

"DAMN it man, let me go, give me back my goddamned shoes and let me go," Bill demanded as he tried to grab onto something to hold so that Frank would stop dragging him along in his thousand dollar suit.

The construction worker simply laughed at his captive's futile efforts.

Then, in a fast move, Frank flipped Bill onto his stomach, grabbed his socked ankles and lifted him high.

"HOLY FUUUUUCCCCKKKK!!!!" Bill screamed as he now found himself seeing everything from an upside down perspective. "FUCKING SICK guy put me down man!!!"

As he was lifted higher by his ankles, with seeming no effort whatsoever, Frank carried the executive up a flight of stairs. Bill's suit jacket dangled behind his head and his trousers rode down toward his knees.

"Nice pretty tall socks Billy bud," Frank laughed as he lugged the executive up the stairs, holding tighter to his socked ankles as he plowed on. "Did the wife buy you these silky numbers, just like that silk tie of yours?"

As Frank ascended the stairs he ran his palms up and down Bill' silk socked calves a few times.

Once up the stairs Frank scurried down a short hallway to what was obviously his and his wife's bedroom. He carried Bill into the bedroom and literally dropped the hapless executive onto the huge king-sized bed. Not knowing what the hell the do, Bill simply lay there in stunned silence. He then watched as Frank stripped off his ratty looking tee shirt, revealing a huge chest, big silver dollar-sized nipples, a washboard stomach region, biceps and triceps that looked like knotted cables and shoulders wider than a doorway.

"Fuck, no wonder he was able to lug me like a sack of laundry," Bill whispered and as he sat up on the bed, Frank grabbed him by the shoulders and literally shucked his suit jacket off him.

The burly construction worker was glad to see real fear now showing in the executive's eyes. Too many times Frank had seen these suit and tie and tall socked guys who thought they were better than him just because they dressed real fancy.

As Bill sat there in continued silence Frank helped himself next to wriggling the executive's tie off him along with his frosty white well-starched button down shirt.

"WH-WHAT are you doing man???" Bill was finally able to squeak out.

But before he even realized what the hell had happened, his hands were tied behind him, with his own necktie at that.

Bill then watched as Frank unzipped his jeans and extracted his gigantic erect cock from them, along with a pair of sweaty kiwi-sized big testicles.

"Oh God, what..." Bill began, but then he suddenly found himself somehow entranced by Frank's HUGE man meat and he could also see from the look in Frank's eyes that the big oaf was impressed with the body he had forcibly revealed under Bill's upper portion of his suit.

"Yeah, that's it bud, I'll bet you NEVER saw a cock and balls like mine eh?" Frank asked, looking at his neighbor's impressive torso.

"Fucker, untie me now!!" Bill ranted as he knelt up on the bed. "This is totally insane here!!!"

But then, to the executive's further shock and total disbelief Frank reached over, pulled Bill to him and slurped one of the executive's nipples into his greedy mouth.

"OH FUCK, what the fucking, fuck," Bill garbled and twisted and struggled in the giant construction worker's grasp.

But pulling away was not an option, as Bill soon found out, as Frank held him TIGHT by his upper arms, and slurped and sucked harder yet at his nipple.

"AW man, I love it when they struggle," Frank said with a grin and quickly slurped Bill's other nipple into his mouth. "Yeah, nice tits bud..."

Despite his struggles and disbelief at what had befallen him Bill found that he had a boner growing in his suit trousers. The executive threw his head back, a feeling of disbelief mixed with ecstasy overwhelming him at that point.

"OH SHIT…SHIT…Frank, Mr. Marone, what in all fucks are you doing to me here???" Bill ranted, looking down and watching as the tit hungry construction worker alternated his tits in and out of his mangy mouth, sucking them, chewing on then, bighting them, teasing the tips of them and mauling the beefy sides of them at what seemed like bionic speed.

The sounds of slurping filled the air of the bedroom as Frank sucked the executive's tits like a madman.

Then, when Bill's tits were swollen, erect and engorged, the construction worker made his way down to his captive's crotch.

"Oh my God, oh my fucking God," Bill whispered and tried in earnest at that point to get his hands untied. "You're a cock sucker; you're planning to suck my goddamned executive cock Mr. Marone."

The construction worker chuckled meanly, pushed Bill down onto his back and yanked his suit trousers off him in one quick pull, and before the executive had time to realize it, his briefs were gone next, leaving him clad now in just his tall navy blue socks. Frank grinned maniacally from ear to ear when he saw the erection that the executive was sporting.

"FUCK, a feast," the construction worker grunted breathlessly. "Never saw a cock so hard, not even on my construction buddies when we all horse around with each other. You're at full mast Billy bud."

"Damn it man, you're looking at my cock the way my wife used to look at it," Bill muttered, backing away from the construction worker as best he could, but it was no use. "Yeah, the way she used to look at it, before things changed, before we became what most married couples become, used to each other…and now you, my goddamned neighbor, the father of the kid who's bullying my kid, has that hungry look for my cock."

Bill then threw his head back and he grunted breathlessly, louder than the construction worker had just moments ago, as Frank slurped his hard cock into his greedy mouth, AND at the same time, jammed a thick finger into the hapless executive's asshole.

"AWWWWWWWW, GAWWWDDD..." Bill seethed and moaned as the construction worker sucked his cock and fingered his shit chute.

"YEAH, gonna eat your meat Billy bud," Frank said and meanly slurped the executive's cock back into his mouth, sucking him harder this time.

"AWWWW you sure as fuck are eating my meat you cock sucker," Bill reeled and squirmed on the bed as Frank slid a second finger inside his hole and prodded him.

"OOOOOO FUCK, I'm cumming man, I'm gonna feed you my executive spunk," Bill grumbled and arched his head back as Frank's fingers gently massaged his ass walls, making him spurt and cum even more. "ARRRRRHHHHH GAWDDDDD..."

When Bill was done feeding the over-sized construction worker his load Frank untied his hands and looked down at him.

"Now, what's this problem our kids are having in school?" Frank asked and the two men grinned at each other.

The Mangy Sheer-Socked Construction Worker

Author: Christopher Trevor

What a day it had been. Fucking ninety-four degrees with one hundred percent humidity. New York was having one of its worst summers for the year of 2012. And lucky fucking me, as a construction worker for the reputed company of Green's and Sons I was fortunate enough to be spending most of it outdoors on a construction project on the roof of and office building in Manhattan. I spent most of my day sweating and stinking like a mangy pig. Yeah, a hairy muscular mangy construction worker, that's what the fuck I am. The only consolation I had for the heat was the money. Good bucks guys, fucking back breaking hard-earned bucks. You see, when the weather was hot or cold in either extreme the workers get paid time and a half. It's a clause in our union contract. Any fucking way, it was Wednesday, the last week of July when *this* happened. Fuck, I still can't believe that *it* happened. I had just completed my ten-hour shift in the blazing hot sun and was headed home on the "F" train to my apartment in Brooklyn. I smelled pretty ripe but thanked God that the train was air conditioned, which covered up my rugged manly scent. I wasn't lucky enough to get a seat for the ride home so I stood holding onto a pole dressed in my sweat sopped light blue tank-top, a pair of well-worn blue Levi's jeans, and black scuffed up lace-up work boots.

Along the way on the train I noticed a couple of faggots checking me out, really fucking drinking in the sight of me, the big muscled, hairy, thick mustached, and mean looking construction worker with the dark brown chestnut-like eyes. I simply glared at them but they brazenly looked at me lustfully. Fucking guys were probably imagining how big my cock was. Fuck, they were probably thinking how great it would be to take a ride or a few on the big construction worker's over-sized sausage meat. One of them couldn't seem to take his eyes off my huge pecs, which just for the record, were bulging, big and straining in my tank-top. As the two faggots stared at me they were whispering comments to each other. Fuck, I felt as if I was on display. Fucking faggots, goddamned butt pounders, they were actually licking their lips in between checking me out and whispering to each other. When they got off the train I was glad to see them go. *Fucking faggots* I thought meanly.

A few stops before mine I got a seat. I sat for the last few stops and I have to say that my body thanked me. I was aching from the long grueling day of slinging two by fours, swinging hammers, and carry cinderblocks in the scorching hot sun. Being that the train was no longer too crowded I stretched my long legs out in front of me. It felt great to do that, let me tell you, sitting there all stretched out like a big side of beef. When I got off the train I decided to take the bus from the train station to the block where I live. It was too fucking hot and I was too damned tired to hoof the more than ten blocks. Besides, I had my metro-card with the free train to bus transfer. That metro-card is one of the better things to happen in New York City over the last ten years or so. Standing at the bus stop with the other commuters I noticed yet another faggot checking me out. Must be my fucking lucky faggot day I thought. I decided to tease this fucker just a little. As he was stealing glances at me I pulled my tank-top forward, making as if to cool myself off.

The faggot looked lustfully at my big brown pointy nipples surrounded by mats and mats of hair on my huge muscular chest.

Fucking faggots, besides being crazy for cock they're suckers for man tits, every one of them. And lucky for this faggot I was giving him an eye-full of two of the biggest, beefiest, and fleshy man tits on the face of God's green earth.

I then lowered my tank-top and hefted up my jeans, accenting my sausage-sized cock in there for him. The faggot looked like he was drooling. I turned my back on him and smiled snidely from ear to ear. Teasing that drooling faggot had really made my fucking day. Then the bus appeared a few blocks off. All the commuters along with myself boarded the bus and after that point I didn't see or think of the faggot I had teased again. But, I had no idea just how much fucking trouble I was headed for that evening. It seemed as though the fates were against me and that I would pay dearly for the little show I had just given the faggot while waiting for the bus.

I got off the bus on my block and walked slowly toward the apartment building I lived in. My thoughts were filled with things like stripping out of my sweat stinking clothes, taking a cool shower, having a hearty diner of take-out Chinese food, and relaxing in my recliner with a freezing cold beer. But unfortunately for Harvey, the muscle-bound sweat stinking construction worker, none of those things would come to pass that night…

As I walked slowly through the warm lobby of my building I was able to catch the musty scent I was giving off. Man oh fucking man, I would need a long fucking shower. I smelled like a locker room after a grueling football game. I took my keys from my pocket and opened the door to my apartment.

"Ah, good to be home," I said out loud as I walked into the apartment and slammed the door shut behind me. "Now for a long shower and... *what the fuck???*"

I stopped in my booted tracks when I saw that my apartment was a fucking shambles. The cushions on the couch had been overturned; books were strewn all over the living room floor, my DVD player was gone along with my television set, the framed pictures that had been on my end tables were on the floor, and my coffee table was turned over also. All the stuff that had been in my glass wall unit was also strewn over the floor.

"Holy fuck, *I've been robbed,*" I blurted out in shock and stepped further into the apartment. "Fuck, my jewelry in the bedroom and that stash of money I keep hidden in my damned sock drawer!! OH NO!!!"

Without thinking that the thief or thieves could still possibly be in the apartment I strode angrily toward my bedroom. I mean, fuck, I'm five feet ten inches tall and built like a brick shit house, what the fuck did I have to worry about? Plenty, as I would soon find out. As I walked through the mess in the living room, reaching for the cell phone in my pocket at the same time, he suddenly appeared from behind the couch and stood in my path. I stopped again in my booted tracks and being that I was tired and really winded from the workday and blasted from the heat my instincts were not one hundred percent.

Before I could do anything he clocked me good and fucking hard across the chin, a real hard packed muscle sandwich landed on me, let me tell you.

"HOOOFFFFF!!!" I grunted, spun around in my boots, tottered stupidly, dropped my cell phone and watched as it slid under the couch, and landed in a sprawl amidst the mess of my living room.

I landed on my back and saw the guy standing over me. Fuck, he was just about my height giving or taking an inch, with wavy brown hair and dark mean looking eyes. He was dressed in worn looking jeans, a faded black tee shirt, and mustard colored work boots.

"Looks like I didn't get out of here in time eh bud?" the guy snickered, towering over me. "Jeez, look at the fucking size of you! Fucking big beefy guy you are!"

"Fucking thief!" I snarled angrily, thinking I could handle this mug with no problem.

As I slammed my big hands against the floor and made to stand up the fucking guy quickly kicked my booted feet out from under me, sending me sprawling again.

"YUHHHH," I gasped as I hit the floor a second time.

"Looks like I'm going to get a little more than what I came here for huh bud?" the guy asked me, reached down, and meanly grabbed a handful of my mussed sweaty dark brown hair.

Fucking guy was stronger than an ox, I'll give him that. He hauled me roughly to my feet by my hair, my big muscular arms flailing at my sides. I roared in bloody agony and before I could even think to do anything to defend myself he punched me hard in the stomach, knocking the wind right out of me.

"OOOOOOOFFFF!!!!" I sputtered.

Holding me tightly by my hair he quickly landed a second hard well-rounded blow to my gut.

"HOOOOFFFFF!!!" I gasped and practically jumped out of my boots.

As I stood there then doubled over in searing pain the guy grabbed me from under my arms and literally flung me across the room. I slammed against a wall and bodily slid to the floor, practically in a stupor at that point.

"OHHHHHHH GAWDS," I mumbled miserably.

"HA! Bigger they are the harder they fall, that is so fucking true!" the guy chortled.

Suddenly, he was behind me. He reached down, grabbed me again by a handful of my sweat soaked dark brown hair and pulled me meanly and painfully back up to my booted feet.

"YAAAHHHHRRRR!!!" I roared in a real guy's pain, my arms again flailing uselessly at my sides, and trying to get my bearings.

I clenched my hands into fists, but again the guy was too fucking quick for me. He turned me around facing him, leaned down and bit hard on one of my big brown nipples, right through my damned tank-top.

"AYYYRRRR GAWDS, another damned faggot!" I seethed and he slammed me hard against the wall, again knocking the fucking wind out of me. "UUUHHFFFF!!!"

Holding me by the handful of my hair the guy pulled me away from the wall and walked me doubled over through my ransacked living room.

"Boy oh boy am I going to have fun with you Tarzan!" the guy laughed, whacked me hard across the kisser and sent me sprawling into the mess all over the floor.

This time I hit my head one of the big heavy legs of my overturned coffee table. I lay there in between consciousness and a stupor. I wasn't sure but it felt as if my tank top was being ripped off me.

"OH man, fucking hairy brute you are Tarzan," I heard the guy saying, as if from far away. "So fucking glad I brought some rope along with me. Looks like I'm going to need it."

When I came groggily out of the stupor I had been knocked and conked into I found myself propped bodily up against a wall in my living room. The guy's knee was pressed strongly against my lower back, just above my sexy rear end and he was just finishing knotting the rope that was looped around and around my upper body.

"OOOOHHH GAUD, what, what the fuck happened?" I rasped miserably. "Feels like a fucking freight train hit me."

My vision adjusted and as it did I saw that I was standing against a wall in my ransacked living room.

"OHHHHH GODS, n-now I remember," I mumbled in despair.

Suddenly, from behind the thief grabbed my big broad shoulders, hefted me up and off my bound up feet (strong fucker he was let me tell you) and turned me around facing him. The bastard got me balanced on my tied up feet and when I looked down at myself all bound up the way he had me a wave of anger mixed with fear coursed through my muscular body.

And to add insult to injury the fucker had stripped me down to my sweat smelling piss stained white briefs and my rancid calf-length black sheer socks. I saw my torn up jeans and my ripped tank-top on the floor. I did not see my work boots anywhere. My briefs were pulled down in the front and back, tucked under my big beefy cock and plum sized juicy balls and the crevices of my well-rounded muscled butt. Actually, my briefs were curled up just under my crotch. My hands were tied tightly behind me at the wrists. Mounds and mounds of rope had been tied over and over my torso and under my huge pecs, pinning my muscular arms to my body and making a nice showcase of my big man tits, causing them to jut out nice and inviting like. My tree-trunk like legs were roped up tight in three places as well; at the thighs, just under the knees, and at my sheer socked ankles. I tottered there on my bound feet as the guy who had broken into my place and ransacked my apartment was sitting on one of the cushions of my couch, which was on the floor and a few feet from where I was helplessly standing. *He had my boots.* One of them was in his hands and he was sniffing heartily at the inside of it.

"OH GAWD, sleazy pervert," I grunted.

He took another sniff of the inside of my boot, tossed it aside and sidled up real close to me, sitting on the floor at my tightly bound sheer socked feet.

"You smell real good and randy Tarzan," the guy snickered, placing the palm of a hand around my socked calf and squeezing hard. "You smell real fucking hot and bothered."

At the moment I was beyond hot and bothered, I was totally fucking pissed the fuck off. I mean, what guy in my position wouldn't be totally pissed off, being that I had been robbed, beaten, stripped to my damned socks and briefs and captured and tied the fuck up in my own home???

Snickering, the goddamned thief snapped the elastic in one of my socks against my iron-like calf. Then, he placed his other hand on my calf and ran both hands up and down and up and down my well-toned legs.

"Jesus Christ on his cross, but you are a big fucking hairy brute Tarzan," he said breathlessly.

"FUCKER, what's the point of all this?" I yelled down at him. "Why didn't you just rob me and be on your fucking way? You have to get the fucking drop on a guy, strip him and tie him the fuck up as well? Take what the fuck you came for and get the hell out of my apartment man!"

"I would watch my mouth if I were you bud," the guy said and this time snapped the elastic in both my socks. *You are in no goddamned position whatsoever to be making any kinds of demands at all."*

"Fucker, untie me and we'll see just how anxious you are to be playing with my damned socks!" I seethed.

"Yeah, speaking of that Tarzan, what the fuck is up with these sheer dainty socks you got on?" he asked me. "The way I figure it, a big smelly construction worker like you would be wearing a pair of thick whites. When I yanked those clonky boots off your big feet and saw these, well, I purposely left them on you before roping you the fuck up the way you are now."

"If it's any of your goddamned business all my thick whites are in the fucking laundry," I replied angrily.

"Heh, heh," the thief chuckled and ran his hands over and over my sheer socked feet. "Oh man, I am really going to have fun with you bud."

Then, with his goddamned mangy hands on my feet he pulled himself to a kneeling position, his face level with my crotch.

"Oh, and as for the jewelry in your bedroom and money that you keep stashed in your sock drawer, I already got all of it," the guy said, looking up at me, his hands on my muscular thighs now.

"Oh fuck man," I said miserably.

"You should have known that a guy's sock drawer is the first place a house thief would look for goods," he laughed up at me, squeezing my thighs.

I then watched in total horror as the guy leaned forward and slurped my soft cock greedily into his mouth.

"OHHHHHH OH GAUD, no, *no man, not this!*" I rasped as the wind was suddenly sucked out of me.

The fucking guy swirled his big tongue all over my cock, suckled his lips around it, and poked his tongue tip into my big wide sexy cock slit. I had no doubt that my cock and balls had to be stinking and rancid from the grueling day I had just spent in the searing sun, they had really sweated up a storm in my briefs and jeans, but this fucking faggot house thief didn't seem to mind whatsoever. Fucking guy was sucking me like a vacuum cleaner turned up real high.

"OHHHHHH FUCK," I moaned as he sucked me up to a good-sized hard-on. "Fucking pervert, goddamned degenerate, sucking my big beefy construction worker cock."

I tottered and squirmed on my tied up feet as the guy ran his hands up and down my legs, toyed some more with my damned sheer socks, and grabbed and squeezed the bejesus out of my melon shaped muscled butt cheeks. With his hands squeezing my butt cheeks hard he gobbled my big meat down into his throat, his face pressed against my thick pubic bush. FUCK, I was sweating now more than before, as the fucker hadn't bothered to turn on the air conditioner in my living room. Fuck, he would probably steal that too I thought miserably.

"OOOOHHH fuck man, I don't believe this shit, *fucking faggot,*" I ranted breathlessly as the thief's tongue again swirled over and over and over my big cock in his mouth. "Not bad enough you had to rob me but you had to tie me the fuck up and suck my big meat too???"

"That ain't all I'm going to do to you Tarzan," the guy said, quickly and greedily slurping my now rock hard cock back into his mouth.

"ARRRRRRHHH no man," I grunted and looked up at the ceiling.

When my cock was beyond hard and throbbing wildly I felt it. FUCK, but I was going to shoot a whopper of a fucking load. I could not believe it; this faggot was actually going to get my nut.

"OHHHHHH man, you-you're getting me there you sick bastard," I whispered huskily and curled my toes back under my sheer black socks. "OHHHHHH GAWD man, I don't believe this shit! What a fucked up day this turned out to be!"

He sucked me faster and harder, really driving me batty.

"OOOOOOOOHHH, GAWD, now, NOW you fucker," I grunted madly and shot my load like gangbusters, right in the sleazy bastard's mouth. "OOOOHHHH fuck, look at you man, just fucking look at you, scoffing down my creamy load...

His mouth felt like an out of control suction device around my cock as he continued to suck me, gulping down rope after creamy rope of my thick sperm.

He moved his hands off my butt cheeks and his fingers teased my big hairy sweat soaked balls. As his damned fingers glided over my sac I erupted still more, spewing a few more globs of ball juice into the guy's mouth. He didn't lose a single drop of it, fucking guy swallowed it all, feasting on my good stuff, GODS!!!

When I was done spewing my mess (and it would be the first of more than a few let me tell you) the guy let my cock slip out of his mouth. It hung there semi hard over my big balls as the guy licked and smacked his lips with his tongue.

"MMMM, you taste sweet Tarzan," the thief said contentedly. "So fucking sweet, I would think at the sight of you that a big brute like you would taste all sour and vile. And I'll bet your girlfriends all love swallowing your creamy mess too."

He took the tip of my big cum slimy and saliva soaked cock between his thumb and first two fingers, held it straight out and looked at it adoringly, as goose bumps broke out all over my musculature at his touch. I was all sensitive and sexy at the cock right now buds. And as he held my cock and looked at it I thought about what he had just said. Any of the girls I had dated had *never* swallowed my creamy load of ball juice.

My thoughts were suddenly cut short however, when the guy slurped my meat a second time into his god-awfully greedy mouth.

"OOOOOHHH GODS man, not again you bastard," I gasped and balled my tied up hands into fists. "Fuck man, I'm all fucking sensitized down there after just shooting a hefty load like you sucked out of me."

Ignoring me the guy again more than sucked my big meat, savoring it in his mouth with his tongue and lips, fuck, he suctioned my cock with that mouth and tongue of his. His lips moved slowly up and down my big cock as his fingers squeezed and tugged at my big sweaty balls.

"OHHHHH you fucker man, *I really don't believe this shit!!!*" I gasped and stood there sopping and stinking in my sweat.

He again moved his hands over my butt cheeks, squeezed them hard, and yanked me forward on my tied socked feet. My cock slid down into his throat and his face was again pressed against my pubic bush. He sniffed my bush and held my butt cheeks tight as he drove me insane. FUCK, I had no doubt at all that I would soon shoot a second hefty load of hot ball juice for the guy. Slowly, he let my cock slide upwards and out of his throat, his lips moving gingerly over the sides of it, his tongue teasing the bejesus out of my slit. I moaned and groaned and hemmed and hawed like a man in heated passion and then, suddenly, I felt it again.

"OHHHHH GOD, you sleazy faggot," I grunted. "Y-you're goin' to get my damned nut again!!"

I arched my bound body back and stood there grunting and groaning as I again spewed my mess into the house thief's mouth.

"OHHHHHH shit, oh fuck!!!" I seethed as he knelt there with his hands on my socked calves and cock only halfway in his mouth.

I seemed to just keep cumming and cumming the way the guy was sucking my cock as I spewed my second goddamned load of ball juice. His eyes were closed and there was a look of outright ecstasy on his face as he scoffed down my construction worker ball juice.

"*Fucker,*" I whispered through clenched teeth as he licked the last droplets of sperm from the crown of my cock, sending waves of chills through me.

I stood there helplessly and shuddered in the unforgiving bondage, squirming miserably under the tight ropes. My cock slipped slowly from his mouth again and he looked up at me as I looked down at him in total anger.

"MMM, I could suck you off all day Tarzan," the guy said and gave my big dangling nut sac a wet sloppy lick.

"UHHHHNNN," I gasped as his tongue glided over my balls. "L-look man, you got what you came here for, why don't you just untie me and leave now?"

"Got what I came for?" the guy asked me, looking up at me, his fingers and thumb curled tightly around my balls. "Tarzan, when you walked through that door I hadn't gotten even half of what I came here for."

"Fuck man, what all are you planning on doing to me???" I asked him miserably, feeling totally helpless and stupid all at the same time.

With a wicked looking grin on his face and my damned balls in his hand he leaned forward and pressed his nose and mouth against my underpants curled up under my crotch, the way he had fashioned them while I had been out cold. He sniffed them heartily and then again ran his tongue over my big balls.

"UHHHHNNN," I groaned.

"MMM, fucking big stinky guy you are Tarzan, now don't yell too loud and I won't have to gag you for this, and the only things I can think of using to gag you with would be those dainty black sheer socks you're wearing," the guy snickered and then slurped one of my nuts into his mouth.

"RRRRRHHHHH GODS," I rasped not too loud, seeing as I too didn't feel like being gagged with my stinking socks, sheer or not, through clenched teeth. "Bastard, sucking and torturing my damned nut, what a thing to do to a poor guy's balls after draining them so forcibly."

With his eyes wide open with glee he looked up at me as he sucked harder and harder on my nut, pulling it hard with his lips, his tongue applying awful pressure to it. I've heard of guys who enjoy having their nuts sucked and eaten, but not me buds, not Harvey, the friendly and being raped construction worker. But there wasn't all that much that I could do to stop him now was there? As he sucked one of my nuts his fingers toyed with, teased and squeezed the other one.

"OOOOOO GOD, easy with my balls you bastard," I whispered huskily.

Then, he switched and slurped my other nut into his mouth, and used his fingers on the one he had been sucking just seconds ago. He alternated back and forth more than a few times with my poor nuts, giving them both equal sucking and torture time. By the time he stopped sucking; licking and torturing my poor nuts the poor guys were swollen and hurting real fucking bad.

MMM, my mouth is really tasting of hot smelly construction worker right now Tarzan," the house thief said, looking up at me and grinning, caressing my damned socked feet as he taunted me.

Damn it all, but my balls were aching. I watched then in agony as the guy reached for a short length of rope and looped it around the base of my cock and just over my poor aching balls. He tied the rope snugly around and around the base of my cock and over my balls.

"OOOOOOOHHHH no man, please, *don't be tying up my damned cock and balls,"* I groaned miserably as painful chills sped through my bound, beaten and muscular body.

The guy tied two knots in the rope on my cock and balls and then slowly got to his feet. He stood there facing me our eyes locked on each other's.

"Fucking big hairy brute you are Tarzan," the thief said lustfully, his hands moving over my big hairy chest and pecs, squeezing them. "You're a feast fit for a fucking king and then some."

I leered meanly at him and he grabbed my nipples with his thumbs and first two fingers. "AYYYYRRRR fuck, you lowlife," I grunted as he squeezed, twisted, pulled, and pinched the fucking fuck out of my big fleshy nipples. "FUCK man; leave my damned tits alone huh???"

With that shit-eating grin on his face he stepped behind me, wrapped his arms around me, pulled me close to him, and again grabbed my big nipples. Again he teased the fuck out of them, squeezing them, twisting them, and pinching them hard.

"AAAARRGGGHH, you fucking bastard," I seethed and tried in vain to get my hands untied. "I swear to God man, I'm going to get out of this and fucking make you pay!!"

I don't see that happening at all Tarzan," the guy snickered and kissed the back of my big bull-sized neck.

"OOOOOOHHH man, I do not believe you just fucking kissed me man!!" I seethed even more now.

As the house thief teased and worked my tits he again kissed the back of my neck, ran his tongue over it, and slurped one of my earlobes a few times. Without realizing that I did it I craned my neck and rested my head on the guy's shoulder. He suckled my earlobe and worked my damned tits, he worked my damned tits and sucked my earlobe, he sucked my earlobe and worked my damned tits, GODS!!!! He really worked and sucked me buds...

"That cock of yours getting hard Tarzan?" the thief asked me mockingly. "You think I can get you so worked up that you'll shoot a third load of ball juice for me pretty soon?"

He suckled my earlobe and worked my tits he worked my tits and suckled my earlobe. And, there was no doubt about it, my cock was growing hard between my tied up legs. Shit, shit, what the fuck was up with all this? Chills sped through my body at what felt like a hundred miles an hour, my nipples, from what he was doing to them, were hard and erect, and fuck man, to my shock, so was my cock. The guy stepped back in front of me and admired the handiwork he had done on my nips. He touched the hard tips of them with his fingertips, sending still more chills through me.

"OH man, I got you all worked up Tarzan," the guy chortled. "Just look at these big titties and that hard cock, all ready to splooge your sludge again I'll bet."

"Y-you bastard," I whispered and the fucking guy leaned forward and slurped one of my very erect hyper-sensitive nipples into that greedy mouth of his.

"AAARRRRHHH, fuck, FUCK, but I've become a faggot thief's buffet tonight," I seethed and involuntarily arched my well-muscled body forward.

The house thief sucked the fuck out of my damned nipple, using his fingers to stimulate and tease the other one at the same damned time. Like with my balls he alternated sucking my nipples and using his fingers on them too, squeezing and twisting and pinching one of them while he voraciously sucked the other one. His saliva dripped down my hairy chest, mixing with my sweat soaked chest hair as he then got around to fucking chewing on my poor tits, really making me crazy with it all at that point. My cock was rage hard and droplets of pre cum oozed and dribbled from my wide sexy slit. The way I was all horned up all over again I wanted to beg the fucking rapist to make me pop my nut again, as what he was doing to me tit-wise was really driving me more than batty. He wrapped his arms around my waist, held me tightly against him, and really ate and chewed the fuck out of one of my nipples. The way my head was spinning and with the forced ecstasy I was feeling I couldn't even tell you if it was my right or left sided nipple that he was presently working on, and really, what the fuck did it matter buds?

I did all I could to stay balanced on my tied up sheer socked feet as the guy really put the screws (and his mouth, his tongue, his lips, his teeth) to my nipples. And by the time he stopped working my nubs they were beyond sore, beyond erect and swollen.

Fuck, looking down I saw that my damned man-sized tits were as swollen as my testicles were, FUCK!!! With his arms still around my waist he looked at me lustfully and breathlessly said, "Fuck man, I can't get enough of you!" and slammed his mouth down HARD on mine.

"RRRRMMMMMFFFF!!!" I roared angrily as he sucked my damned tongue into his mouth and fucking kissed me and kissed me and kissed me.

His lips pressed against my thick mustache. He held me tighter at the waist and it felt like he was planning to suck my tongue right out of my mouth. I screamed bloody murder into his mouth buds. When he finally stopped kissing me he looked at me in twisted ecstasy.

"Fucking beyond hot guy you are Tarzan," the guy quipped and pressed his mouth against mine again...and to my utter astonishment I found myself responding to his kiss this time....

When he stopped kissing me again the house thief squatted down in front of me and slurped my throbbing python of a cock into his greedy mouth for a third go round.

"OOOOOOOO GODS," I gasped loudly as his tongue worked it's evil magic on my cock.

I was actually thankful that the goddamned house thief was sucking my cock this time. The way he had teased and tortured my nipples had really sent me into what I'll only call a heated frenzy. And as he sucked me like a madman and tugged on my tied up balls I realized that I would have a lot to think about when this was all over. When it would be over though was anybody's guess at that moment. Fuck, the guy sucked my cock like crazy, running his lips generously and un-sparingly up and down the sides of it, he poked his tongue tip into my slit, and when he deep-throated me and sniffed my pubic bush I felt as if I would jump right out of those smelly sheer socks I was wearing. Goddamn it all, but there was NO denying that the faggot thief was driving me batty. As he sucked me some more I thought about the two faggots I had seen on the train and the one at the bus stop. Fuck, I thought, I bet this is what those three guys would have loved to be doing to me right about now. But then, my thoughts were again cut short when I felt myself getting close to the bursting point, FUCK, I was about to shoot a third fucking load. My poor aching cock tingled like crazy in the guy's mouth...AND then it happened. I shot a load big enough to choke a horse.

"OOOOOOOOHHHH GODS, shit man, you fucking degenerate, got me spewing my mess all over again!!" I grunted, looking down at the guy as he held tightly to my sheer socked calves and scoffed down my juices, my cock halfway in his greedy mouth.

I gyrated and was sweating profusely by then.

"YOU FUCKING sleazy faggot!" I swore downwards at him.

Once again he did not lose any of my jazz. He scoffed every drop of it down, and oh so heartily at that. When he was done I stood there catching my breath as he snapped the elastic in my sheer socks playfully against my calves.

"You know Tarzan, looking at these big ol' smelly sheer socked feet of yours just gave me a really mean idea," the guy said and got to his feet in front of me. "Let's go to your bedroom."

That said he meanly kicked the side of my calves good and fucking hard, toppling me, causing me to lose my balance. I grunted in pain, but before I could hit the floor he caught me and hoisted me up to one of his shoulders.

"UUUHHRRRR," I gasped as my tied-sheer socked feet left the floor.

With his hand resting on one of my ass cheeks he lumbered with me toward my ransacked bedroom.

"Fucking low-life thief, SCUM you are, put me down man!!" I roared angrily. "Fucker, carrying me like a sack of laundry or something!!"

In my bedroom he dumped me onto my bed, flat on my back. I was totally fucking helpless as he grabbed my socked feet and propped them up atop my footboard at the end of the bed.

"What in all fucks are you planning to do to me now man?" I asked him angrily, watching intently as he handled those sheer socked tootsies of mine.

Then, he left me lying there and dashed back to the living room. While he was gone I tried again to get myself untied, tugging and pulling at the ropes around my wrists. But alas, it was no use, the bastard had tied me too fucking tight and even all my strength could not help me at that point. I looked down at my stinking sheer-socked feet propped up on my footboard and I wondered what in all hell he was planning on doing to me now. The sleazy faggot house-thief had already gotten the drop on me, stripped me to my damned socks and tied me the fuck up. And woe of fucking woes he made me shoot my damned load three times by sucking the fuck out of my big meat stick, and tortured my damned nips to force me along with that, JEEZ!!!"

Looking up at my tied up feet atop the footboard a feeling of dread coursed through my muscular sweaty body…

Then, he returned a few minutes later, with a small brown bag in his hand.

When I looked at the bag in wonderment the house thief said, "Got everything I'll need right here Tarzan." He grinned at me and held up the bag. I watched as he placed the bag on the bed next to me.

"What the fuck are you up to now man?" I asked him meanly. "Why don't you just get the fuck out of here already?"

"Oh no, not for a while Tarzan, not for a long while," he said, moving toward my feet. "I have too many things in mind to do to you. You're simply a smorgasbord of sexual feasts."

That said he untied my feet, my knees, and my thighs. I struggled like crazy as he pulled one of my socked feet to the end of the footboard and began retying it at the ankle, tightly to the footboard.

"F-FUCKER!!" I ranted at him, squirming miserably on the bed as he tied my foot tightly to the footboard.

"Figuring it out huh Tarzan?" he asked me, turning to face me with a devilish looking grin, his hand gripping my now tied foot.

"I am going to fucking tickle torture you till you're beyond crazy with it. Then I'm going to tickle torture you some more. And then after that I'm going to tickle torture you some more, and more…"

"OH GODS," I muttered and lay my head back down on the pillow, knowing all too well just how very ticklish I am.

The thief then grabbed my other foot, pulled it over to the other side of the footboard and tied it off at the ankle to the footboard as well. The lower part of my body was now spread out and completely visible for the antics he planned to visit on me. I wondered despondently what was in the bag he had dropped on the bed next to me. When he was done tying my other foot to the footboard he stood menacingly over me.

"Hate to do this to you Tarzan, but I need you to be out of it for a few minutes while I get you spread out like a cheap whore," he said and grabbed a handful of my hair.

"AAARRHHHH!!!" I roared as he yanked my head up by my hair.

He gave me a hard mean rap across the face, sending me into a semi stupor.

"UUUHHNFFFF," I gasped and the room spun and turned blurry in front of me.

When I came out of the stupor a few moments later my face was hurting where the bastard had clocked me…AND…I found myself now tied in a full spread-eagled position. My upper body had been untied and my wrists pulled up and tied off at the ends of the headboard. My damned underpants were now off me and they were sticking out of the back pocket of the thief's jeans. I guessed he was going to keep my stinking briefs as a souvenir of all this, fuck, add my damned briefs to what he had already stolen I thought miserably. As I woke up fully I realized what a really fucked up and heinous position I was now in, tied to my own bed in a spread-eagle position with just my smelly sheer socks on. The rope that had been tied under my cock and above my balls was gone. My sweaty and stinking balls were resting on the bed, still hurting from the suck job the guy had given them earlier. My cock hung soft and shriveled over my aching gonads.

"You awake?" he asked me, looking down at me and coming clearer into my line of vision.

"Y-yeah, I think so," I said softly. "Fuck man, you've got a punch like a goddamned freight train."

"I'll take that as a compliment," he said and held up two clip-on clothespins for me to see.

"Promise not to scream too loud and I won't gag you," he said and squeezed the clothespins open.

I realized that they were clothespins from the bag I kept under the sink in my kitchen. Sometimes I would wash socks and underwear in the sink and hang them up in the bathroom to dry. But oh fuck; I NEVER thought that those clothespins would be used for this shit as the house thief moved them close to my swollen and very erect nipples.

"OH God, *no man, no, please,*" I sputtered, lifting my head up off the bed and looking fearfully at the clothespins as he brought them closer and closer to my poor nipples.

Then, with a fast clip my nipples were encased in the tight clip-on clothespins.

"AAAYYYYRRR GODS!!!" I seethed through clenched teeth and bucked furiously on the bed. *"Fucker, get those things off my damned tits!"*

"Not for a while Tarzan," he said teasingly and stood up straight.

He spent a few seconds watching me buck around in the tight bondage, no doubt my musculature arousing him all the more. Then, with a mean and wicked looking grin on his face, he walked over to my left bound socked foot.

"Now, let's see just how ticklish you are big boy," he said and glided the tip of a finger over the meaty bottom of my left sheer socked tootsie.

"OOOHHHHH GAWDS, n-not this. not this you bastard, oh please man," I gasped and squirmed miserably on the bed.

He then glided two fingers over the bottom of my left sheer socked foot, sending tickling chills through me. I loudly guffawed and bucked wildly then on the bed.

"AAARRRHHH SHIT, SHIT, ha, ha, ha, ha, ha, ha, ha!!!" I laughed uncontrollably as he trailed and trailed his fingertips over and over the bottom of my left foot in circles. "OH you bastard, stop this now!!! Stop this now man!!!"

"Just as I thought, a real ticklish construction worker," the guy said meanly and leaned down over my foot that he was tickling.

I watched as the sleazy fuck slurped at the tips of my sheer socked toes and continued to tickle me at the same fucking time.

"OOOOOHHHHH, OH GOD, ha, ha, ha, ha, ha, ha, ha, ha, fucking sleazy bastard, sucking my stinking toes!" I laughed crazily, gasped, and bucked up and down on the bed. "PL-please man, please, *d-don't tickle me!!*"

My cock was getting hard again and bobbing real sexily against my body as I flailed wildly on the bed, as the guy tickled my damned foot more and more.

The clothespins on my nipples also bobbed around, driving me crazy with pain as they pulled and tugged on my poor clipped tits.

"AAYYYRRRR SHIT, I am goin'-going to make you pay fucker!!" I seethed. "Somehow I will make you pay, ha, ha, ha, ha, ha, ha, ha, ha, ha!!!"

He stopped tickling my left foot and stopped sucking my toes, only to quickly move over to my right foot.

"Don't want this big smelly foot to be feeling lonely do we now?" the house thief asked me and pressed two fingertips against the bottom of that foot next.

"OOOOOHHHH PL-please man, st-stop this, please," I begged desperately. "Ha, ha, ha, ha, ha, ha, ha, ha, ha OH SHIT, this is too much!!"

I lifted my head up off the bed as he slurped my socked (right) toes into his mouth and sucked them hard, tickling the beefy bottom of my foot at the same time.

"UN-untie me you fucking bastard!!" I said demandingly. "OH FUCK, OH GODS, ha, ha, ha, ha, ha, ha, ha, ha, ha, ha!!!! OOOOOOOO..."

I fell back on the bed as he applied torturous pressure to the bottom of my foot with his fingertips, moving them around in a circular motion. I was sopping in sweat from head to my socked toes. When the guy moved his thumb over my arch I nearly went totally crazy.

"HA, ha, ha, ha, ha, ha, ha, ha!!!" I guffawed loudly and insanely. "OH MY GODS, not there man!!"

Seeing that he had found a definite weak spot he meanly zeroed in on it, using two hands and all his fingers to tickle the arches of my feet alternately. I bobbed up and down and flailed like a fish out of water on that bed, screaming, laughing and going insane with it all.

In between tickling my big smelly feet the fucking guy sucked my socked toes, chomped on my heels, and slobbered over the tops of my feet, quickly slurping up his saliva. My poor nipples were in a pain I had never known before, and un-fucking-believable, but my cock was rage hard as I bobbed and bucked madly on my bed.

"OOOHHHHRRR GAWDS," I seethed, sweat dripping off me everywhere by then.

What a lather I was in buds...

Finally, oh finally, he stopped tickling my feet, but I knew I was still in for more nastiness. As I lay there catching my breath he stood over me, looking down at me hungrily.

"Feeling good Tarzan?" he asked me and tugged on one of the clothespins on my nipple.

"OWWWWWWWW, shit, yeah, I'm feeling real fucking good," I growled angrily at him. "Just what the fuck I've always wanted, to be kidnapped and tied tighter than a drum to my own bed and tickle and tit tortured! Yeah, I'm at the top of my fucking game right about now fucker!!"

"Thirsty?" he asked me with a grin.

"A-actually, yeah, I am at that," I said to him.

With a mean looking leer on his face he pulled down the zipper on his jeans, extracted his long semi-hard meat stick, and climbed up on the bed. He straddled my upper body and pressed the tip of his cock to my trembling lips.

"Drink up big boy," he said meanly. "Slake your thirst."

"Y-you have got to be joking man," I said beseechingly, my lips grazing the tip of his cock as I spoke. "Y-you're going to make me scoff down your damned piss??? That wasn't what I had in mind when I said I was thirsty."

"You said you were thirsty guy," he said to me, pushing his cock head over my lips and rubbing it against them. "And beggars can't be choosy now, can they?"

With a look of horror in my eyes I took the tip of his cock in my mouth, closed my lips tightly around it, and he instantly began pissing. I was fucking thirsty as hell and I found myself, to my utter shock, gulping down his rancid piss *and* sucking his damned cock.

He looked down at me adoringly as I drank and drank his piss, sucking his cock like a damned nursing baby. When he was done pissing he let his cock slip out of my mouth and climbed down off the bed.

"You fucker, *you sleazy faggot!!! You goddamned lowlife!!!*" I ranted at him as he packed his cock back into his jeans. "What kind of sick fuck are you to make me drink your damned vile tasting piss???"

He simply chuckled, picked up the brown paper bag, and reached into it. When he brought out my portable high-speed electric toothbrush I nearly screamed in fear and laughter, knowing all too well what he was planning on doing with it.

"OH NO, no, please man," I gasped pleadingly, thrashing madly on the bed as he walked over to my left foot.

The thief clicked the toothbrush on to top speed and the hard bristles whirred to life.

"OH GAWD, no, no!!!" I begged as he grabbed the top part of my foot to hold it still.

Then, he pressed the vibrating bristles against the bottom of my left foot.

"*Ayyyyyrrrrrrrrr shit, shit, shit, ha, ha, ha, ha, ha, ha, ha, ha, ha!!! Oh shit, th-this is too fucking much now!!*" I screeched loudly as he ran the vibrating bristles over and over the bottom of my foot.

Once again I bucked wildly and thrashed around on the bed. When he moved the bristles over the arch of my foot I was too winded to scream, instead I simply heaved and laughed and laughed and heaved on the bed. He moved over to my right foot and tickle tortured that one next with the damned electric toothbrush, MY own electric toothbrush. And that was only the beginning of his tickle tortures that he had in mind for me with my damned electric toothbrush. Never before had the sounds of my toothbrush whirring been so ominous to me. Holding my left foot tightly in his grip he then ran the vibrating bristles of the toothbrush over the balls of my foot and the very tips of my socked toes. I was racked with uncontrollable laughter and pain as I bucked still more on the bed. The thief grinned from ear to ear as I lay there heaving as he ran the toothbrush back and forth and back and forth over the tips of my socked toes.

By the time he stopped tickling my feet with the electric toothbrush I was out of my fucking mind with laughter. I lay there sopping wet in my sweat and trying desperately to catch my breath. The house thief turned off the electric toothbrush and squatted next to me. The ropes around my wrists had loosened a tad and he quickly went to work reinforcing them, tightening them up, insuring I would not escape.

"F-f-fucker," I whispered, stifling a bout of laughter. "H-haven't you had enough sick f-fun with me?"

"Enough?" he asked me. "Tarzan, I haven't had this much fun in a long fucking time."

With that he pulled hard on the rope around one of my wrists and it was again taut. He did the same with the other rope on my other wrist, and then moved down to my feet. Looking down at myself I saw that my cock was indeed semi hard and twitching between my legs. As the guy reinforced the ropes around my feet I was moving my crotch area up and down on the bed. Big mistake buds, HUGE! As I hefted my crotch area it gave the fucking thief a good bird's eye view of my gaping ass hole.

"OH man, have I come up with a really mean and sick fucking idea now Tarzan," the guy said and quickly jumped to his feet.

I watched in tortured agony as he again grabbed the electric toothbrush. He clicked it on to high speed and the sound of it whirring to life filled me with dread.

"Okay you big fucking lug, for this *I am going to have to gag you,"* he said meanly and tucked the whirring toothbrush under his arm.

"WHOOOO, that sure as hell does tickle Tarzan," he said gleefully. "I sure am glad that I'm not the one all tied up and being mercilessly tickle tortured, HA!!!"

I then watched as from my sock drawer he took a pair of my OTC black socks, seeing as dress socks were all I had in that drawer, seeing as all my thick white sweat socks were in the wash, as I had told the house thief earlier when he had questioned the reason why I was wearing the sheer numbers under my work boots that day, JEEZ. One of the OTC black socks he wrapped into ball and crammed it as deeply as possible into my danged mouth, the other he tied over the one in my mouth. Fuck, the only consolation I had at that moment was that he hadn't gagged me with the socks I was wearing. He preferred those to remain on my feet anyway.

"RRRMMMFFF!!!" I sputtered angrily.

Then, once I was effectively gagged, he climbed up on the bed, straddled my stomach area with his back to me, and when he started moving the electric toothbrush slowly into my gaping asshole I knew why he'd had to gag me.

"RRRMMMMFFFFFFF!!!!!" I screamed in bloody agony.

He teasingly moved the vibrating bristles of the toothbrush slowly over the walls of my hole. My head spun, my vision blurred, and I sputtered like mad behind my socks gag. I bucked around on the bed and beads upon beads of my saliva slid out of the sides of my gagged and stopped up mouth. When he moved the toothbrush deeper into my hole I lifted my head up off the bed and screamed at him through the gag.

"RRRMMMMFFFFFFF!!!!!" I garbled loudly as the sick fuck tickle tortured my hole.

He grabbed my cock, held it straight up, yanking my balls up as well, and swirled the electric toothbrush around and around and around in my gaping and sweat stinking raunchy-filled hole.

"MMMMMFFFFF, mmmmmmfff, *mmmmmfffffff,*" I laughed behind the damned socks gag.

My hole was tingling like mad as he slipped the toothbrush deeper and deeper into it. He moved that damned whirring device in and out a few times, fucking my poor hole with it, and then he moved it over the walls of my hole again. I thought for sure that I would go completely and utterly out of my mind at that point. But then, OH GOD, then, as he went on and on torturing my hole with the whirring toothbrush he began stroking my meat stick.

RRRRRRRMMMMFFFF!!!" I gasped, knowing that with the way I was so hard I would have no damned problem shooting yet another load of spunk for the thief.

I balled my tied hands into fists, curled my toes back under my sheer socks, and squeezed my eyes shut, trying oh so fucking desperately to endure the tortures being inflicted upon me. The vibrating bristles of that toothbrush in my hole were painful and ticklish at the same time. I stupidly thought how I would not brush my teeth with that brush again.

"OH yeah, I'll bet that this hole of yours is feeling real good right about now Tarzan," the guy quipped and stroked my meat faster.

My thoughts were again cut off as I felt my balls cooking up another batch of my spunk, and I was getting ready to shoot my load again.

"RRRRMMMMMM!!!!" I sputtered, chewing on the dammed sock crammed in my mouth and stretching my tied arms and legs. "MMMMFFFFF!!!"

The guy sensed it, quickly pulled the toothbrush from my hole, got down off my stomach area, squatted over me, and greedily slurped my cock into his mouth. He again scoffed down my construction worker load of cream.

"MMMMMFFFFF!!!" I sputtered as I shot my load and shot my load like crazy.

The guy had a look of sheer ecstasy on his face as he gulped down my juices. The electric toothbrush was still in his hand, turned on and whirring, teasing me, mocking the fuck out of me...

When I was done shooting what was my fourth load the house thief let my aching and spent cock slip from his mouth. I bucked wildly and thrashed like a madman on the bed as the pain from the clothespins on my nipples had suddenly intensified about one hundred percent... after I had shot my load. FUCK, FUCK, every damned part of me was sensitive to the touch at that point.

The fucking guy was really doing a number on me that was for sure. I gasped loudly and in agony when he slipped the vibrating toothbrush back into my hole.

When he finally stopped tickle torturing my hole with the electric toothbrush a little while later I was a tingling, sweating, and turned to jelly mess, and as he pulled the toothbrush from my hole, sliding it over the walls of it, I had my torso in the air and I was squirming miserably.

Long lines and droplets of saliva dripped from the sides of my gagged mouth and beads of piss were now dribbling from my cock and onto my stomach area. Oh yeah, I was a mess all right. When the toothbrush was out of my hole the guy squatted next to the bed, pressed two fingertips against my big chest and lowered my torso back down.

"Mmmmmmffff," I whimpered, turning my head and looking at him beseechingly.

He reached over and jiggled one of the clothespins on my nipples, sending blinding and searing pain along with chills through me. My muscular body was awash with goose bumps as he ran his fingertips through the floods of sweat all over my chest and stomach. I watched as he then licked and sucked his fingertips.

"MMM, as I said, you taste so fucking sweet Tarzan," the guy panted. "Seeing you like this and working you over this way is *really* making me horny bud."

All I could do was simply look at him angrily; being that I was gagged there wasn't all that much I could say after all. He put my electric toothbrush on the night table next to my bed, as I lay there spread out like a side of beef. I watched miserably as the guy began stripping off his tee shirt. His body was that of a runner, lean and lanky. Fuck, that a guy like that was able to get the drop on a big built strong fucker like me, mortifying. In moments the guy was stripped to a pair of thick white sweat socks pushed down around his ankles. Smiling wickedly he picked up my electric toothbrush and clicked it on. A look of helplessness filled my eyes and I choked back tears.

"Heh, heh, bet those tits of yours are feeling real good right about now," the guy snickered. "I just bet that they're in need of some real attention, huh Tarzan?"

As he climbed on the bed and straddled my lower body I nodded my head furiously "NO" from side to side, knowing all too damned well what I was in for now as he took the clothespins off my nipples.

"RRRRMMMMMFFFFFFFFF!!!!!" I roared as the blood rushed furiously back into my poor nipples at what felt like a thousand fucking miles per hour.

The guy wasted no fucking time; I suppose being a house thief caused that in him. He quickly pressed the whirring bristles of the electric toothbrush against the tip and sides of one of my swollen, overly erect and highly sensitized nipples.

"MMMMFFFFFF!!!!" I screeched and bucked on the bed under his weight.

"Oh yeah Tarzan, going to ride you like a fucking white pony," he chortled as he moved and glided the toothbrush over my other wrecked nipple. "Going to fucking ride you like a fucking bronco."

As I bucked and thrashed under him, to my disbelief, my cock grew hard again, as he tickle tortured my poor nips with that blasted electric toothbrush of mine. My teeth were tingling and I chewed meanly on the socks gag. As my cock grew still harder and I felt his hole gliding over it I looked up at him in wonderment, astonishment and outright fucking rage.

"RRRRMMMMMFFFFFFF!!!!" I gasped as his hole began to slide onto my pole. "HHHHRRRRRMMMFFF…"

"Oh yeah, big fucking brute wants to fuck my hole," the thief panted and held the whirring toothbrush against the tip of one of my nipples, sending hot searing pain through it.

"FR-FRUCKER," I gasped incoherently as his hole slid down fully onto my shaft.

His creamy butt cheeks were sitting on my crotch and I have to fucking admit, man, that it felt all warm and squishy in that hole of his.

"OHHHHH yeah," the guy panted and gyrated in a man's passion on my meat stick, again moving the toothbrush back and forth and back and forth over and over my nipples. "Fuck me you beefy bastard!"

Unbelievable even to myself I began thrusting inside him, really fucking his tight hole. Fuck man, it felt better in there than any pussy my big cock had ever been in. I again clenched my tied hands into fists, curled my toes back under my sheer socks, and squeezed my eyes shut. I fucked and fucked the guy like crazy as he ran that toothbrush over my nipples. I couldn't fucking believe it, I had scoffed at faggots on my way home from the job-site that night and now there I was, fucking lashed to my bed being tickled at the tits and fucking pounding some faggot thief's squishy tight hole. It would not be long before I shot a good hefty load of construction worker ball juice into that hole. I had cum so much already that night, but the way this guy had me so worked up and over the top hard, FUCK, I KNEW I would cum again for him. The thief bounced up and down on my cock, fucking torturing the shit out of my poor, poor nipples.

"OH YEAH, fucking hot construction worker you are Tarzan," the guy panted gleefully and sadistically. "Fuck, I think I'm going to stay here all night working you over!"

I looked up at him angrily and rammed my cock harder and harder into his damned hole, wanting to hurt him, but instead he seemed to enjoy it all the more.

"OHHHHH YEAH, fuck me you scruffy bastard," he said demandingly.

I fucked him like crazy and he slid up and down on my damned cock. Then, after a long while more of him torturing my tits and raping my cock with his hole, I felt it, I was going to fucking shoot my damned load again. I couldn't believe it buds; I had never shot my load so many times in such a short period of time. But this bastard of a house thief torturing me sure knew how to get my nut every fucking time he wanted it.

"RRRRMMMMMFFFF!!!" I sputtered with my eyes squeezed shut and shot my load into the thief's hole.

"OH yeah, that's it Tarzan, fill my hole with it," he gasped and stroked his hard cock at the same time.

When I was done shooting my mess in his hole he didn't get up off my poor spent cock, instead he kept sliding up and down on it and went on as well running the electric toothbrush meanly over my now beyond sore nipples. That really drove me fucking crazy let me tell you. My cock was all slimy and sensitive as he rode it semi hard, stroking his cock for all he was worth at the same time, FUCK, and still torturing my nips.

"RRRRRmmmmmffffff, *fr-frucker,*" I seethed, lifting my head up off the bed.

Smiling meanly at me he wagged his hard cock in my face.

"Oh yeah, you drive me crazy Tarzan," he teased me. "Just looking at you all stripped and roped the fuck up is enough to drive me nuts, but having your big tool inside me *really fucking gets my nut!!*"

Then, he clenched his teeth and leaned forward, (sliding off my cock) tossed the electric toothbrush aside, and yanked the socks gag quickly out of my mouth. Before I could utter a damned word he jammed his cock halfway in my mouth and forced me to chow down on his cum. And without realizing what the holy fuck I was doing I moved my lips up and down over his shaft, gulping down his creamy hot spunk…

"OH yeah, drink it, swallow me you big gorgeous hunk," he gasped breathlessly.

After he was done shooting his load he kept his damned cock jammed in my mouth. FUCK, I didn't need three guesses to know what was next. With a loud sigh of contentment he pissed in my mouth a second time. He shuddered on top of me as I drank down his piss, suckling at the tip of his cock. When he was done pissing he slowly, almost reluctantly pulled his cock out of my mouth. I lay there with my head lifted and my damned tongue hanging out, the taste of his cum and piss overwhelming me. He mockingly rubbed the tip of his cock on my tongue a few times, cleaning it off it seemed, all while looking down at me adoringly.

"Fuck man, I actually think you're starting to enjoy all this shit I'm heaping on you Tarzan," he said as I lay my head back down.

"N-no way fucker," I rasped meanly as he climbed down off the bed. "Fuck, fuck you; I'm not enjoying any of this humiliating shit. Tied the fuck up, stripped to a pair of my damned stinking socks of all things, being tortured, MAN, this is not my idea of a good fucking time!"

Smiling, he strode to the end of the bed and leaned down over one of my tied sheer socked and by now beyond stinking sweaty feet. He grabbed it tight in the middle and gave my toes a few good hearty sucks.

"UHHNNNN," I gasped as chills crept through me. "OOOOOO man, look at you, you pig now, sucking my damned cheesy socked toes."

I tell you, above all the other things he had done to me AND would do to me; he seemed to be totally obsessed with my feet, and the fact that I was wearing those silly sheer black socks. I watched as he sucked my cheesy toes through those sheer stinkers I had on, a look of sheer (pardon the pun buds) ecstasy on his face. Frankly, I was afraid he was going to start tickling me again. Actually *he was going to tickle torture me again,* but it wouldn't be my feet this time. Oh no, he had other parts of my big muscular body in mind to torment the fuck out of next. My poor nipples were still hot and tingling from the grueling workout he had given them with the electric toothbrush.

After a while he stopped playing with my foot and sucking my toes. But to my dismay he retrieved the damned clothespins and I watched in sweaty agony as he clipped them AGAIN onto the tips of my nubs.

"OHHHHHHH GODDDDDD!!!!" I screeched madly.

He picked up the brown paper bag, reached into it, and produced two long stick-thin paintbrushes.

"Oh shit, what now you bastard?" I asked him miserably, trying to deal with the new pain in my nipple tips as I spoke. "You've had your fun torturing and raping the fuck out of me, why can't you just untie me and be on your merry way, huh?"

Without a word he stood next to the bed, leaned down, and began tickle torturing me with the paintbrushes. He stuck the stick end of one of them into one of my hairy armpits and began twirling it and running it around in there.

"OOOOOOOOOHHHH SHIT, oh fucking shit, ha, ha, ha, ha, ha, ha, ha, ha ha!!!!" I gasped loudly. "OH NO, oh no, not this, not my damned pits!!!"

As he tickle tortured my armpit with one of the damned paintbrushes he ran the bristles of the other one over my stomach regions. Once again I bucked, thrashed, and squirmed miserably, like a fish out of water, on the bed. My laughter turned into loud heaving gasps and the clothespins on my nipples bounced up and down, tugging unforgivingly on my poor nip tips. (Rhyme not intended.)

"Y-you sick fuck," I wheezed as he really put the screws to my hairy very ticklish armpit. "TH-this is sick torture!! HA, HA, HA, HA, HA, HARRRRRR!!!!"

Goosebumps broke out all over me as he slid the bristles of the other paintbrush all over my stomach area. When he slid the stick of it into my bellybutton I was sure that if I weren't tied to the bed I certainly would have flown right up to the ceiling.

"OOOHHHHHHHH, AAYYYYYYY, GODDDDS," I screeched in a high pitched tone of voice. "I swear man, I swear, you will pay, ha, ha, ha, ha, ha, ha, you will pay dearly for all of this!!"

Then, the ultimate humiliation happened. He slid the bristles of the paintbrush that he had been using on my stomach region into my hole and twirled it around in there, tickling the walls of my hole like crazy.

"Oh God no, no," I panted and pissed on myself, spurting it out of my cock in long hearty droplets. "OHHHHHH GAWD."

"Oh man, look at that, just look at that mess," the thief said and stopped tickling me. "Now for that you really need to be taught a hard lesson."

He yanked the clothespins off my nipples and before I could scream and rant in pain anew he quickly crammed one of my black OTC socks deep into my mouth.

GAWD, I had pissed myself. The last time I had done that I was five years old and in kindergarten. But now, at thirty-four years of age it truly was the ultimate humiliation. Actually, everything this faggot house thief had done to me, and would do to me, was the ultimate humiliation for a construction worker dude like me.

As I lay there totally helpless, drenched in sweat and piss I watched as the house thief untied my feet from the headboard. I didn't know what the fuck I was in for now, but fuck; at least he had stopped tickling me. (Temporarily? God, I hoped not.)

"Okay bud, time to get you up and off that bed," he said and yanked my head up by a handful of my hair.

"UUUHHHMMMFFF!!!" I gasped in pain and he rapped me a good hard one across the old kisser. "MMMMFFFFFF!!!!"

He let go of my hair and as I fell backward again I was stunned, too damned stunned to do shit as he untied my wrists from the bed board. He pulled me to a seated position on the bed and quickly retied my hands behind my back.

GAWD, my face was going to be a mess of bruises and swelling come the next day, what with all the times he'd clocked and socked me. With my hands now securely tied behind me he hoisted me up and onto his shoulders and lumbered out of my bedroom. The sock gag fell out of my mouth as I dangled over his shoulders and he trudged along with me.

"F-fucker, *p-put me down,*" I whispered, still in the stupor he had clocked me into.

I found myself in the kitchen, with him of course, a few minutes later. As I came around I found that he had slumped me over my heavy wood table on my stomach, with my sheer socked feet dangling just inches off the floor. My upper body was securely roped down to the table and mounds of rope had been tied around and around just under my ass cheeks, making a real nice sexy showcase of my melon-shaped globes. I watched miserably as he rummaged through drawers in the kitchen, taking out a plastic spatula and a wooden spoon. GOD, I thought in total misery now, I was about to be spanked like some misbehaved child.

"Weren't you taught years ago never to piss on yourself Tarzan?" the house thief asked me mockingly, setting the wooden spoon down on the table in front of me but holding onto the spatula.

"M-my fucking name is Harvey, n-not Tarzan, you blasted thief," I muttered, sweat from my hair dripping onto the table.

"Looks like you need to be taught *a really hard lesson,*" he said, sneering down at me.

Dressed in just his thick white sweat socks he stepped behind me with the spatula in hand.

"Damn, what a piece of ass you got, Tarzan," he said breathlessly and gave one of my ass cheeks a hard squeeze. "Like a fucking bowl of whipped cream."

Then, he brought the spatula down HARD on one of my ass cheeks, really laying his strength into it.

"YOWWWCCHHHH!!!" I snapped. "BASTARD!!!"

He rapped my ass cheek a second and third time, real hard. Stinging pain shot through me and he gave my ass cheek another three hard whacks in quick succession.

"RRRRHHHHHH..." I ranted through clenched teeth as he began spanking my ass cheeks alternately with the plastic spatula. "Y-you fucker!!"

I tried not to yell out all that loud, hoping that he would not gag me. The clean socks that he had used to gag me with earlier were back in my bedroom and the only socks available to gag me with were his or the sheer stinkers I was wearing. GOD, and I did not relish that thought, I mean, gagging a guy with a pair of stinking socks is a really shitty ass thing to do to him, know what I mean buds? The fucking house thief spanked me harder and harder with each goddamned blow, and before long I knew that my poor ass cheeks were turning red.

"ARRRRRHHHH GODDDDD," I snarled crazily as he held one of my stinging ass cheeks in his fingers and thumb and really pounded the other one with the spatula.

Sweat was dripping all over me again and tears of rage and pain were filling my eyes. I couldn't help it; the fucking pain had become beyond intense. He spanked me and spanked me and spanked me on the ass.

"Bet you wish I were still tickling you eh Harvey me boy?" he asked and whacked my ass cheeks again and again and again, the sound of that spatula ringing maddeningly in my ears at that point.

It was the first time he had called me by my proper name.

"ARRRRRHHHH, *pl-please man, PLEASE,*" I sputtered as tears slid down my face.

"Ha, got the big macho muscled construction worker crying like a fucking baby," the guy chortled meanly and rapped my by now crimson ass cheeks still more with spatula.

I squeezed my tear-filled eyes shut, clenched my teeth, and seethed in pain, anger and outright humiliation. He stopped whacking me with the spatula about fifteen minutes or so later. I was shaking and trembling under the damned tight ropes and crying, fucking crying like a goddamned baby. Actually I was crying because I watched as he put the spatula down and picked up the long-handled wooden spoon.

"We're not done yet Harvey me boy," he said to me mockingly.

The damned thief stepped next to me, grabbed one of my butt cheeks tightly in his fingers and thumb, and with his other hand brought the wooden spoon down on my other ass cheek.

"AAARRRRHHHH," I cried out. "Mangy bastard…"

I struggled fruitlessly under the binding ropes as the house thief whaled hard into my butt cheeks with the wooden spoon. I lay my head on the table and again clenched my teeth. Again, I tried not to scream out too loudly for fear of being gagged with his or my own damned socks. With a wicked grin on his face he alternately beat my poor wounded ass cheeks with the wooden spoon. Stinging and searing pain sluiced through me at what felt like more than a hundred miles an hour. I was feeling like I would literally go insane at that point, the things he had done to me, what he was doing to me, I was beyond feeling angry and humiliated. I did not know anymore what the fuck I was feeling.

"EEEEEYYYYRRRR, shit, SHIT, en-enough of this already man," I ranted desperately. "Y-you've had your twisted fun with me! Now get out of here and leave me in peace!!"

He stopped spanking me, grabbed a handful of my hair and yanked my head up off the table.

"Leave you in peace?" he asked me. "Leave you, leave you? Tarzan, I'm just getting going on you."

That said, he let go of my hair and quickly resumed spanking my ass cheeks, HARD, with the goddamned wooden spoon. I shuddered violently under the ropes, taking in what he had just said to me… What the fuck else did he have in mind for me???

A good while later the house thief stopped spanking my ass cheeks. I could feel that they had welts on them and were beyond crimson. Fuck, I would have placed money bets on the fact that you could have fried a couple of eggs on those ass cheeks of mine at that point. But even though he had stopped spanking me I wondered miserably what he had planned for me next. Damn it buds, I didn't have to wait all that long to find out. "Oh man, first I beat your ass, now I'm going to eat your ass," he said to me as he quickly undid the ropes holding my upper body to the table. Eat my ass???

"OHHHH GAWD, you sleazy pervert!!" I grunted from the throat.

Within a few moments I was fully lying atop my kitchen table. He had crossed my arms up behind me, one atop the other and roped them tightly together in three places. My legs were spread wide apart and dangling off the sides of the table, exposing my gaping bung hole. FUCK, he had me spread out on my own table like a goddamned Thanksgiving feast and my ass was about to be the main course. Standing behind me and leaning down the guy ran the palms of his hands over my crimson spanked butt cheeks, squeezing and kneading them hard. He leaned down further and ran his mangy tongue over them a few times. Unbelievably, it felt great, him licking my ass cheeks, what with the horrendous spanking he had just administered to them. My cock tingled and started to get hard underneath me. Then, with his hands on the cheeks of my ass he spit liberally and generously into my hole a few times, soaking and sopping me up back there for a good chow down.

"Oh man, what a piece of beefy ass you are and have Tarzan," the guy muttered and began by flicking his tongue tip over the walls of my hole.

"OOOOOOOOOO shit," I mcaned, not wanting to admit how awesome it felt, what he was doing to me.

With his hands on my cheeks he spread them even further apart, opening my doors to his paradise. His tongue flicked over my saliva soaked hole and teased the fuck out of me.

"OHHHHH my GOD, fucking raunchy thief you are, lapping at my stinking mangy asshole," I grunted.

He buried his face in my hole and tongue fucked it. GOD, unbelievable but true, his tongue was working a twisted sort of magic back there. The thief swirled his tongue tip in and out of my raw pungent and stinking hole, making my head spin. Actually, my head had been spinning since he first clocked me and all this craziness had begun.

"OHHHHHHH man, what a night this turned out to be," I grunted madly.

He salivated in my hole, sucked it up, and tongued me more and more and more back there. He ran his big hands up and down my thighs, squeezed them, spanked them, and tugged meanly on the hair on them as he feverishly lapped and licked my hole. At one point he puckered his lips in there and sucked at it.

"HUUUUHHHHHRRRRR," I gasped, lifted my head up off the table, and my eyes crossed in my head. "F-fucking heathen, slimy raunchy bastard you are…"

He spit again into my hole, getting it newly moist and again set his tongue to work in there. There was no denying it that I was hard as stone at that point. My cock pounded and throbbed under me. I broke out in a hot and most stinking sweat buds.

"Oh yeah man, got you in a fucking lather," the guy said after he had stopped eating my hole.

He stood up straight behind me and with no damned warning, jammed two fingers into my sopping wet hole. Then again, why would he have to warn me about anything he was going to do to me? Who was the one tied the fuck up after all?

"EEEEEeeeeeeyyyrrrrr, SHIT, get your danged fingers out of my stinking hole you bastard!" I ranted angrily.

Ignoring me, he sank his fingers deeper inside me, prodding around in there as if he were digging for gold. Chills coursed through me and goose bumps covered me from head to toe under the sweat.

"Oh man, what a hole you got here Tarzan," he quipped and slipped a third finger inside me.

"AAARRRHHH, GAWDS," I ranted as his fingers slithered around in my hole.

"Fucking going to return the favor you gave me earlier," he said and yanked his fingers out.

Then, before I knew what the fuck was happening he was up on the table behind me, his hard cock jutting out in front of him. I could not fucking believe it, but I was about to be fucked up the ass like some cheap whore.

"OOOOOHHHHH no, no, *not this you bastard,*" I seethed as I felt the tip of his cock starting to make its way into my hole.

I rolled my hands into fists and clenched my teeth as he slid deeper inside me, his cock rubbing my ass walls and stretching me open to accommodate him.

"OH yeah, yes, oh fuck yeah, tight as a fucking clam," the thief panted. "Going to pop your cherry Tarzan, going to stick my cock up your ass and fuck the tar out of you."

He slid his manhood home and my hole felt like it was literally filled with his big tool. He began thrusting in and out of me, holding tightly to my hips, squeezing and kneading them.

"OOOOOOHHHHH, RRRRRRRRR, goin' to kill you for this you scumbag," I garbled and because of the pain my head spun away.

He chuckled loudly and spanked my crimson ass cheeks.

"Kill me?" he asked and slammed his rod deeper yet inside me. "Harvey ol' boy, you're going to fall in love with me."

"I'll be damned if that's going to happen!!" I retorted and he again grabbed my hips.

"OH yeah," he panted as he slipped and slid in and out of me like crazy.

I heard the sounds of squishing as his cock slid in and out of my hole, it was a maddening sound for me. I curled my toes back under my sheer black socks and the bastard fucked me and fucked me and fucked me and then he fucked me some more. GAWDS!!!!

"OHHHHHH fuck, getting close you hot fuck, you stud of a construction worker Harvey me boy," he panted. "Going to fucking fill you to the brim with it."

Then, for the second time that night the thief spewed his mess, but this time right into my stinking shit chute.

"OOOOHHHHH yeah, YEAH, fucking cumming in your damned mangy hole you mangy sheer socked construction dude," the guy sputtered and spanked my wounded ass cheeks hard.

I felt his warm juices flooding my hole as he spewed his second big mess of slop. It seemed to go on and on, as if he would never stop cumming.

I sarcastically thought how great it was that I could have that effect on a damned gay house thief. When he was finally done he sprawled atop me with his shriveling cock still buried deep inside me. He kissed my huge shoulders and I choked back tears of rage and utter humiliation.

Slowly, so slowly, his cock slid from my hole and after he had caught his breath he climbed down off the table. Leaning down he gave the bottoms of my sheer socked feet a few hearty sniffs, licks and kisses.

"Tell you what Harvey ol' boy of mine," the guy quipped and squeezed my big feet. "When I do finally leave here I'll be taking these stinking socks of yours with me too. Them and your underpants will make a nice souvenir of all this."

"Fucker you are man, you can have my damned socks and under shorts," I muttered angrily. "Just please, *please,* get the fuck out of here and leave me be. Goddamn it man, you're more than tortured the fuck out of me."

"HEH, heh, that's just it Tarzan, I can't seem to get enough of torturing the fuck out of you, you sure can fucking take it, that is a given," he chortled and rapped my ass cheeks hard.

"ARRRRHHHHH, shit!!" I grunted and then the thief was on the table again behind me.

His cock had grown hard again and he quickly and uneremoniously slid it deep into my hole a second time for another good go round.

"OHHHHHHH, FUCK, FUCK," I raged as I felt him fill me and stretch my poor ass walls out once more.

"Yep, that's it Harvey me boy, *fuck,*" he panted and thrust hard in and out of me.

"OHHHHHH GAWWWWWD, my poor hole," I grunted miserably as he rammed me hard again and again.

I kept my teeth clenched, my big hands balled into fists, and my toes curled back under my socks and wondered miserably how something like this could have befallen me.

"OHHHHHH man, oh yeah, great fucking hole you've got Tarzan," the guy muttered and whacked my ass cheeks over and over as he fucked me and fucked me. "Getting there soon bud."

Then, after a while more of really fucking the tar out of my hole the guy erupted with another torrent of ball juice. He spewed another good-sized load of cum into my hole, flooding it.

"OHHHHH YEAH, fucking A you muscle bound fuck!" he seethed and seemed to cum and cum endlessly in my hole, spanking my ass cheeks and squeezing them hard.

When he was done his cock slipped slowly from my hole. Shuddering and catching his breath he climbed off the table. Then, standing behind me he pulled my ass cheeks painfully apart and plunged his tongue into my gaping well-fucked hole. Like an animal in heat he licked and lapped at my hole, eating and slurping his cum out of it, spitefully taking back what was his.

"OHHHHHH GAWWWD," I grunted and chills sped through me anew. "Fucker you are, eating my damned raunchy hole again."

It drove me crazy as his puckered lips sucked at my hole, his tongue tip teased it, and he moved his hands up and down the backs of my big hairy thighs. After he'd slurped all his mess out of my danged hole he ran his tongue over my ass cheeks a few times each, squeezing my thighs at the same time. I panted and grunted atop that table. I wondered just how much more the fucking guy planned on doing to me…

About fifteen ass licking minutes later I found myself standing in the kitchen with my arms still roped up behind me.

The bastard had blindfolded me and I was standing with my legs slightly parted as he squatted in front of me, sucking my big cock and tugging and teasing my balls. My head was spinning, I was drenched and stinking with sweat and my poor body was aching miserably from all the damned tortures he had heaped on me.

"OOOHHHH GAWDS, sleazy bastard, sucking my cock after it's been up your damned shit chute," I grunted breathlessly as he ate my manhood with real gusto.

He ran his hands up and down my muscular tree-trunk like legs, snapped the elastic in my sheer socks and greedily gulped my cock down, way down, and into his throat.

"OHHHHHHHH SHHHHIIITTT," I panted and threw my head back, my blindfolded eyes looking up at the ceiling as he sucked me and sucked me. "Faggot!!!"

Before much longer the guy sucked another good and hefty load of construction worker slop out of me.

"OOOOHHHHH, shit, got me cummin' like a bitch in heat, stealing my good stuff again," I gasped as he gulped down my damned ball juice.

I had lost count at that point of just how many times the fucking thief had gotten my nut. When I was done spewing my mess down his throat he took a few last licks at the tip of my cock, sending chills through me. By then I was so blasted and so tired that I didn't bitch or moan when he took the blindfold off me and slung me up and over one of his shoulders and carried me back to my bedroom…

In my bedroom he dumped me on my bed and I watched as he opened a backpack that was his and took out a big fat pink butt-plug. I had heard things and seen pictures of butt-plugs that my construction workers buddies had found in sleazy magazines. I never once though entertained thoughts of having one used on me. My buddies and I always joked about how faggots loved having the damned things rammed in their butt holes. The thief climbed on my bed, pushed my legs apart, and without a word quickly jammed the damned butt-plug in my hole.

"OOOOHHHH SHIT, what is this now???" I grunted miserably. "Do you always walk around with a damned butt-plug in your backpack???"

Smiling meanly at me, he clocked me hard across the face for what seemed like the fucking umpteenth time. I was knocked quickly into unconsciousness.

When I awoke it was the middle of the night. I didn't know what the fuck time it was because the fucking thief had stolen my digital clock from my night table. My arms were untied and I pulled myself to a sitting position on my bed. I felt the butt-plug still in my hole but made no move to pull it out. I turned on the lamp on my night table and looked around my room. He was gone, I hoped upon hope. God knew I couldn't stand anymore of his hijinks' at that point. Looking down at my feet I saw they were bare. True to his word he had taken my black sheer socks. I slowly stood up, my cock jutting out hard in front of me, GAWDS!! I grabbed my erection and stroked the guy till I spewed a dry load, seeing as I had no more ball juice to shoot, not with how many times the damned house thief had me splooge. When I was done I ran a hand over my hairy chest, sending chills through myself.

Then, I reached behind me and pulled the damned butt-plug out of my hole. It came out with squishy sounds and I farted loud when it was fully out. I dropped the damned thing on the floor and walked to the bathroom.

Standing over the sink I threw cold water over my bruised and battered looking face.

"OH man, fucker really did a job on me," I whispered, looking at my reflection in the mirror. "Swear to God I'll find him and kill him for this!"

I swigged a mouthful of Listerine in my mouth and squished it around in there.

I knew I would have to call the police and report the burglary, but how much I was going to tell them I didn't know yet. Still disoriented and slightly dizzy I walked on my bare feet to the kitchen to get some ice for the bruises on my face. According to the clock on the wall in the kitchen it was three thirty AM. GAWDS, the fucker had put the screws to me for hours. I wrapped a few ice cubes in a dishtowel and pressed it against a couple of the bruises on my face. I then walked slowly back to my bedroom. When I entered the bedroom the first thing I realized (to my horror) was that the butt-plug was not on the floor where I had dropped it after I had yanked the thing from my hole.

"H-holy shit," I whispered, slowly moving the wrapped ice cubes away from my face.

From behind I was clocked hard on the head.

"HOOOOOFFFFF," I gasped and went sprawling into the bedroom the rest of the way and landed in a heap on the floor.

When I came to again I found myself sitting in my bathroom, sitting in the bathtub actually. The tub was filled with hot water and my hands were securely tied behind me. My feet were also tied now and I was gagged with one of my sheer socks crammed deeply in my mouth and the other one tied over it, jamming it firmly in place. My eyes filled with horror and dismay as I realized the guy still had me trapped.

"Oh good, you're awake," he said to me as he knelt at the side of the tub, soaping me over with a washcloth, running it over and over my aching body.

"RRRRMMMMFFFF," I sputtered angrily as I chewed on my rancid socks and he brazenly washed me.

"Heh, heh, didn't think I had left you did you Tarzan?" he asked me mockingly and squeezed one of my nipples, twisting it.

"RRRRHHHMMMFFF…" I wailed as he mashed my nipple hard.

"Oh no, not yet, not for a while, I won't leave you just yet," he went on. "That is for sure. It sure was fun watching you jack yourself off with that butt-plug wedged in your sweet hole. But now I have new plans for you. Got you soaking in hot water to soften up the hair all over your beefy muscular body, because I am going to give you the longest and biggest shave of your life."

I leaned my head back, squeezed my eyes shut for a moment or two, and choked on my tears of utter frustration over all of this, and he washed me, stroked my nipples, and tugged on my now VERY sore cock under the water. Misery and outright despair engulfed me as I realized that this fucking guy REALLY did have me trapped and that I was a total prisoner in my own home.

After I had soaked in the warm water and been thoroughly washed down the guy strung me up by my wrists to the shower curtain above the tub. My muscular arms were spread wide, exposing all the areas of me that he planned to shave. As the water drained out of the tub he applied mounds upon mounds of my shaving cream to my upper body, my armpits, my thighs, my legs, and my entire crotch area, including my hairy and sexy nut sac. My cock grew hard as his hands moved and roamed over me, caressing me as he smoothed the damned shaving cream all over my well-toned muscled body.

"Looks to me like you're enjoying all this after all Tarzan," the thief said mockingly, giving my hard but sore cock a squeeze and twist.

I furiously nodded my head "no" from side to side.

"When I'm done shaving your front side I'll turn you around and do your other side," he said, picking up my long sharp straight razor. "It'll be a pleasure to shave that hairy butt of yours. Now hold still."

He began by shaving the thick mat of hair from my robust chest and pecs.

He swirled the razor carefully around my big nipples.

"MMMMMFFFF..." I muttered angrily.

"Yeah, I bet those sheer socks of yours taste great eh Tarzan?" he asked me as he shaved my chest. "Wow, you really are a hairy fucking brute Tarzan."

He snickered as he held one of my nipples tight in his fingers and thumb as he shaved around it, sending cold chills through me.

"It looks like it's going to take more than one lathering to get you done," he said and ran the water in the sink to rinse off the razor.

I felt a deep sense of loss as I watched my chest hairs sliding down the drain. Once the razor was cleaned off he resumed shaving me, dragging the razor stealthily over my stomach region and around and around my belly button, the feelings of it causing me to break out in goose bumps. I watched intently, wondering what the fuck I would tell the guys at work. With a hand on my side the thief slowly shaved my stomach area. Hairy ol' Harvey was slowly being turned into hairless ol' Harvey, GAWDS!! Then, with a hand on my ass he ran the razor over one of my thighs...and as he squatted there my aching and hard cock stared him in the face.

"God almighty, I just love this cock of yours Harvey me boy," he whispered and gave my meat stick a few sucks.

"MMMMFFFFF!!!" I sputtered, still holding still as he shaved my thighs.

Every time he ran the razor under the water to clean it, and I watched my body hairs go down the drain my heart broke. Within a half hour or so my chest, pecs, stomach, thighs and my legs were all hairless. When he had ordered me to place one of my feet up on the side of the tub I had no goddamned choice but to do as I was told. The thief held my ankle tight as he shaved my lower legs and calves. He gave my bare foot a few licks and sucked my toes a few times as well. My sore cock grew harder and throbbed mightily in front of me. When he shaved my crotch area he ordered me to remain very still. I didn't need to be told twice buds. Holding the tip of my cock in his hand he shaved away my pubic bush and then slowly and oh so carefully shaved the hair off my nut sac. Unbelievably, my cock pounded and throbbed as he shaved my crotch area. I said my prayers as that razor moved over my sexy nut sac. Then, the thief was done shaving my crotch.

"Okay Tarzan, now I'm going to shave those bushy pits of yours," he said as he got to his feet. "It'll probably tickle a bit, so be sure to hold very still. I don't want to cut you after all."

We looked into each other's eyes and for a moment I didn't know what the fuck I was feeling for the blasted thief. When he pressed the razor against one of my pits and slid it across in there it did tickle a bit. But I stayed still as he had again ordered me.

"MMMMMFFFF..." I whimpered miserably as my armpit hairs were shaved off me.

When he was done the front part of my body was completely hairless. But nonetheless he lathered a second coating of shaving cream all over me.

"GAWDS," I miserably said to myself. "Here we fucking go again."

Actually, I think he was just getting off running his hands all over me, smoothing the shaving cream all over my well-muscled body a second time. Teasingly, he tugged on the rancid socks in my mouth and gave my newly formed erection a few twirls. I bucked my body forward and whimpered.

"Want to shoot another load eh Harvey me boy?" he asked me. "Soon dear boy, soon."

Then, for the second damned time he began shaving my chest and pecs, getting rid of the stray hairs he missed the first time.

By then my arms were sore and aching from having been tied and spread out for so damned long. When he finished shaving my front side again, instead of untying me and turning me around he climbed into the tub behind me. I shuddered and twitched as he rubbed shaving cream over my huge broad and hairy back, my ass cheeks, and the backs of my thighs and legs. I nearly jumped out of the tub when he jammed two fingers up my ass.

"RRRMMMFFFF," I gasped.

"Oh yeah, going to fuck you good again very soon Tarzan," he said and began shaving my hairy back. "This ass of yours is too tight and too good not to fuck again."

Chills sped through me as the razor glided over my back. He kept a hand on my shoulder to hold me steady in the tub as he did the chore of shaving me. When he got down to my ass I could feel him looking at it adoringly as he shaved the hair off my melon shaped globes. When my ass cheeks were hairless he put the razor down, spread my cheeks apart, and licked and lapped at my hole a few times. You would think that by then I would have been so used to it but it still made me nearly jump in the air. The sensations of his tongue as it glided over my ass walls were indescribable.

A while later he was finished shaving me, both front and back. He positioned himself behind me and jammed his cock deep into my hole again.

"RRRRRMMMMFFF," I gasped as he rammed hard inside me.

He wrapped his arms around my body and hugged me close to him as he thrust in and out of me like mad. He tweaked my nipples and moved his mangy hands down to my crotch. Grabbing my hard aching cock he stroked it as he fucked me and fucked me. I could tell that he was planning on us shooting our loads together this time... AND WE DID.

After he had fucked me and fucked me and fucked me more than I thought it was humanly possible he exploded like a volcano in my hole, flooding me yet again with his juices. AND, I watched as my cock exploded tiny spurts of cum, all of them landing on the floor.

"RRRRRMMMMFFFF, UUUUMMMRRFFFFF," I gasped loudly in a mixture of pain and twisted ecstasy, my head spinning, my vision blurring as I came and came.

"OH YEAH, pop that load you hunk, fucking A!!" the thief snarled in my ear.

After we were both spent his cock slid out of my hole and he quickly squatted behind me to lick my hole cut, taking his sweet time about it, savoring the taste of my cum slicked ass walls. I gushed and gasped like a mad man; felt like I had gone over the edge of crazy, my eyes squeezed shut and pissed into the tub. The thief stood up behind me and again clubbed me hard over the head... The world went black.

This time when I came to I was sitting in the empty tub. My sheer socks were out of my mouth...and gone I wondered if he was too this time. With my head pounding with pain I pulled myself to my feet and climbed out of the tub, glad to be untied once again, wondering if he was still stealthily sneaking about somewhere, ready to overpower and tie me up again for his sick pleasures. My hairless reflection in the full-length mirror startled me. I could not believe how I looked. Inwardly I was glad he hadn't shaved off my mustache. I stepped carefully out of the bathroom and didn't detect the house thief anywhere in the apartment. Still, with every step I took I quickly looked behind me. I did not feel like being clocked over the head again. I had enough bumps and lumps from him to last me a while and God knows I'd had enough of that. When I got to the kitchen I dashed to the phone and dialed 911 to report the robbery...

Before the police arrived I had pulled on a pair of green shorts, a black tank-top and rolled the OTC socks that the house thief had gagged me with earlier onto my feet and up to my calves. The cops arrived pretty quickly and I gave the two young officers a condensed version of what had happened. I told them how I had come home from work to find my apartment ransacked. I told them how the thief had still been there and how he had clocked me across the face, stunned me, and tied me up. I told them that he had worked me over by beating on me and really roughing me up. I didn't tell them of how he had gotten my nut more than a few times, how he had tickle tortured me, how he had spanked the tar out of me, and he had out-rightly raped and tortured me. My body was starting to itch from having been shaved. The blond cop's next question startled me a bit however when he said, "Did the house thief visit any sexual advances on your Sir?"

Sitting across from the two cops in my living room I nervously crossed one of my socked feet across my knee.

"Uh no, I was actually afraid that he might, I have heard of things like that, but no," I said, trying to sound convincing, although I don't think the two cops believed me for a second.

I then gave them a description of the thief and a listing of what I could tell that he had stolen. I didn't mention my sheer socks that I had been wearing that he had stolen as well, it was just too humiliating buds.

The cop with the dark hair told me that they would be in touch if anything came up; they shook hands with me, gave me their business cards and left. As for me, as for poor hairless ol' Harvey, I was exhausted, beyond tired and wanted nothing more than to go to sleep. But, as I was headed for the bedroom the phone rang. I quickly snatched it up and before I could say a word I heard him laughing at the other end.

"Heh, heh, heh, missing me yet Tarzan?" he asked me mockingly. "Is that asshole of yours itching for my cock again?"

"Y-you fucker," I muttered into the receiver and slammed the phone down.

I made sure that all the windows were locked as well as the door before heading off to bed and some very much needed sleep.

Needless to say I called in sick the next day to catch up on sleep. I didn't get out of bed till after one PM. I went to the local diner to treat myself to a hearty brunch and I ate like I hadn't eaten in days. But God, my body was still tingling in spots and I was itchy as all hell from the big shave. When I got home from the diner I cleaned and re-organized the apartment as best I could.

The next day I wore a regular pull-over white tee shirt to the job atop the office building we were working on. Wearing that instead of a tank-top kept my hairless torso covered. I really didn't feel like answering questions from my work buddies as to why I was now hairless. The bruises on my face had gone down somewhat and were not all that noticeable in the hot sun. Before getting started my supervisor called out to me and I saw him walking toward me with another guy following behind him.

"Harvey, I want introduce you to a new man on the job," my supervisor, Jim, said to me as he approached.

The guy behind Jim stepped up to me and I nearly jumped out of my boots, one of the pairs he hadn't stolen.

"Harvey, this is Leo, Leo, meet Harvey," Jim said and I found myself shaking hands with the house thief.

"Good to meet you Harvey," the guy said with a warm and the most innocent looking smile.

"Leo will be your new assistant Harvey," Jim said as Leo still held tightly to my hand.

"Uh, yeah, yeah, cool," I muttered.

"Okay guys, I'll let you two get acquainted, Harvey, show Leo the ropes and I'll check on you guys later," Jim said and walked away.

As Leo held tightly to my hand the expression on my face turned to outright rage.

"H-how?" I asked softly.

Leo snickered and said, "While you were out cold I checked your wallet and found your work ID. I figured I would apply for a job so I could be near you...and here I am. I am a certified steel worker after all. Robbing houses is just a way for me to score extra income."

As he spoke my hand shook in his tight grasp. I nearly blanched when he said, "Now come on Tarzan, the man said you have to show me the ropes. I'll show you some more ropes tonight when we get back to your place." He finally let go of my hand and we stood there staring blankly at each other.

"Fucker you are, I want all my stuff back," I said to him through clenched teeth.

"Sure thing Harvey me boy, as I said, I'll be over tonight," he said and squeezed one of my pecs. "You can count on it."

Then, he looked down at my booted feet and asked, "You wearing sheer socks again? I know you couldn't have done laundry already, not after all the great sex I treated you to."

I simply and stupidly nodded "yes" and he smiled evilly...

We got to work...

Timmy Backman and
his assistant Chad

*Author: Timmy Backman and
added onto by: Christopher Trevor*

It was late in the evening on a weekday, and Tim Backman was sitting at his desk at work completing some correspondence on his laptop. The banking lawyer's suit coat was hanging behind the door to his office, his tie was pulled down, his dress shirt was open by several buttons undone at the collar and his shirt sleeves were rolled up. Timmy, as most people called him, had kicked off his tasseled loafers and had his feet up on his desk so he could comfortably wiggle his toes in his thin executive style black socks. The handsome executive was relaxing after a long day as he clicked away on his laptop.

As Timmy was finishing up his work there was a knock at his office door. He looked up in surprise as Chad, his assistant, strode into the office.

"Chad," Timmy said with surprise. "What are you doing here? I didn't know you were still here. In fact I didn't know anyone was here but me. I thought that you, along with everyone else was gone by now. Look at the time bud."

Chad smiled and walked around Timmy's desk, planting himself next to where his boss man's suit pants legs rested on the desk, him sitting sort of sidesaddle right next to where Timmy's executive socked feet were resting and crossed at the ankles.

"Oh, I knew you would be working late this evening and I just wanted to take this opportunity to speak with you," Chad said and looked down at Timmy's crossed ankles. "You see, I have something to discuss with you and I purposely waited for everyone else to leave."

He then brazenly reached out and plucked at the toe of one of Timmy's executive socked feet.

Timmy looked at his own socked feet, thought about how much trouble they had gotten him in over-time and gulped as he watched Chad's fingers pick at the sock material where his toes then automatically wiggled at the feel of his assistant's touch.

"Speak with me?" Timmy asked. "Chad, you could have spoken with me any time today, during regular business hours..."

Timmy's voice trailed off as Chad pulled a little more on the toe of his sock, rubbing the material between his fingers and thumb.

"But Timmy, Mr. Backman, Sir, it's a private matter and I felt that it warranted a private conversation," Chad announced with conviction. "Nice socks by the way."

Timmy suddenly felt a tad uncomfortable... Timmy...Chad never called him Timmy around the office. The only time Chad had referred to him in such a familiar way was when... "Oh my God..." Timmy said to himself. The only time Chad had been so chummy and familiar was the day that John had hidden under Timmy's desk and taken advantage of him and when John and Chad had managed to strip him naked, all while John controlled poor Timmy through his cock.

Timmy, as most people know is a slave to his cock, and John had taken control of the executive's cock, and then, when Chad had become aware of his boss's secret, about the under the desk blowjob, he had joined in and participated in Timmy's stripping and sexual humiliations. But that's a whole other story, and, that was the last and only other time that Chad had been so brazenly familiar with his boss man Timmy, his immediate superior AND supervisor.

Timmy gulped again and a little moisture formed along his upper lip and his cock stirred in his suit pants, as a result of the sock plucking that Chad was doing at his very sensitive feet. Besides being a slave to his cock, Timmy was exceptionally ticklish, especially at his feet.

"Private matter... whatever could be so private Chad that you needed to corner me, uh, I mean, stay so late?" Timmy nervously questioned.

But to Timmy's shock, Chad simply continued plucking and pulling on his boss man's sock as he observed a concerned and actually weak look form on Timmy's face. Chad knew that Timmy was the boss, but when it came to the boss man's libido, well, the tables seemed to turn in the assistant's favor.

"Why Timmy, I wanted to speak with you about my salary!" Chad said, smiled and actually squeezed Timmy's big toe now.

Timmy gulped yet again and his cock stirred even more as he felt his toe being squeezed. But, he thought to himself, "I'm a vice president in this bank, a banker and a lawyer. I'm Chad's boss...I am HIS supervisor. I should not be feeling nervous, but dang it all, I am!"

"Salary?" Timmy questioned, trying to put a little more authority into his voice. "Chad, you know very well that salaries are not addressed until the fiscal year end and..."

But Timmy's voice trailed off as Chad rolled his big toe between his fingers and thumb...and Timmy's cock actually started to stiffen at the sensation running up from his toe.

"Yes Timmy, I know when salaries are NORMALLY addressed, but I think that I have been doing such a stellar job for you and the bank that you should make an exception and move my raise up to now! Don't you agree?" Chad said, sounding very confident.

"No Chad, I'm sorry, it is a bank and my policy that we only address salary issues at the year end, and…" Timmy was trying to say, trying to take a stand and uncrossed his ankles as if to get up.

But Chad reacted quickly, quicker than Timmy had any chance of reacting himself to the movement. Because Chad jumped up on the desk, sat on Timmy's legs, and pinned them to the desktop.

"Chad!! What the fuck do you think you're doing?" Timmy thundered, suddenly shocked back into his supervisory attitude.

"Timmy!" Chad said from his perch, pinning Timmy's wiggling legs to his own desk. "Isn't there something that I can do to change your mind and bank policy and have you grant me my well-deserved raise?"

Chad was grinning like a Cheshire cat.

Struggling unsuccessfully to dislodge Chad from his legs Timmy replied through straining teeth.

"No Chad, there is absolutely nothing you can do to change bank policy and my mind," Timmy ranted.

But then, suddenly, Timmy froze, his eyes went wide and his lips formed a perfect "O" at the sensation of a finger trailing down the sole of his executive socked clad foot. Timmy swallowed hard as a chuckle bubbled up from his abdomen…then there was a second chuckle.

"CHAD!!" Timmy spoke with a voice that already sounded like fear. "Chad! WHAT, hee, hee, NO, OH NO…don't do that. HEE, HEE!!! Leave my sock, I mean, leave my foot alone. CHAD PLEASE! OH hee, hee, hee, hee…"

The chuckles were beginning to string together as Chad began a little scribbling motion of his fingers on Timmy's socked soles.

Timmy's cock, which had already been awakened by the foot touching, sprang to a full erection in his suit pants. As most people know, Timmy has this agonizing problem, this situation with his cock.

Although he hates, can't stand, cannot tolerate, being tickled, his cock reacts with feverish excitement whenever the banking lawyer finds himself in a tickle pickle. And this was most definitely one of those tickle pickle times. Timmy thought that it might have something to do with his underlying submissive nature that he seldom ever let's be seen...outside of his own bedroom. Another problem for Timmy is the fact that at this moment he was not wearing any underpants.

It's totally another story, but Timmy has recently gotten himself involved with an online Master as part of his masturbation control therapy, and that resulted in his being denied regular orgasms and a pledge not to wear underpants...in other words, to go commando. This aspect of Timmy's life is covered in the cum-less Timmy story, written by Christopher Trevor.

But, back to the present predicament for our Ticklish Timmy, for he was beginning to cackle as he begged Chad to stop tickling his socked feet. But the sounds of Timmy's laughter only egged Chad on all the more and Chad WAS REALLY getting into the action of scribbling his fingernails up and down Timmy's big wide size twelve soles. And lo and behold, Timmy's cock was fully inflated and creating a huge tent in his slacks by then. This had not gone unnoticed by Chad.

"Pleeeeeeeeease...hee, hee, hoo, hoo, hoo, OH CHAD, stoooooopppp!!!" Timmy begged breathlessly. "OOOOOOOOOOO, hee, hee, hee, hoo, hoo, hoo, hooo, iiiiiitttt tiiiiicckles soooooooo much. HEE, HEE, HEE, HEE, HEE, HEEEEEE..."

Chad simply giggled and eyed Timmy's tented crotch.

"Well boss, the rumors are true," Chad said. "You really are the most ticklish man I've ever met. And not only that but you really seem to enjoy it...just look at your pants."

And with that Chad reached over with one hand and grabbed the peak of the tent in Timmy's pants...and squeezed...

Timmy's eyes crossed and the electricity of Chad's touch on his cock surged through his body.

"OH FUCK, hee, hee, hee, wha…wha…no, no, dooooooooo hoo, hoo, hoo this too meeeeeeee, hee, hee, hee, pleeeeeeeeease Chad, sto…sto…stop!!!"

But Timmy simply continued to cackle and beg his assistant to stop the torment. But, as is predictable for anyone who gets the chance to tickle handsome Timmy, he was relentless; in fact, he increased the tempo of scribbling his fingernails on Timmy's executive socked feet… AND began tugging on the silky material at the sock toe, in order to bare Timmy's sexy male feet.

It didn't take Chad long to pull Timmy's black executive socks off his feet, baring his big white ticklish tootsies. Chad's fingers then danced up and down Timmy's soft and oh so sensitive soles.

Timmy cackled and screamed, he was beside himself, trapped in his own office and being tickle tortured by his direct assistant. Timmy's toes splayed and wiggled and his feet moved in vain attempts to avoid Chad's evil fingernails. But all Timmy could do was hang onto his chair and vibrate violently, laugh uncontrollably and beg Chad to stop.

"EEEEEEEEEEEE hee, hee, hee…AAAAAAAAA, ha, ha, ha, ha, ha, ha, ha…oooooooooooo HOO, HOO, HOO, Chaaaaaaaaaaad, hee, hee, hee oh plleeeeaaaaase stoooooooop."

"Well," chad replied with a smirk. "Are you ready then to grant me that raise I so richly deserve? Huh Timmy?"

"NO…NO…you, hoo, hoo, hooo, hooo, you know, hee, hee, hee, hee, hee, you know I can't do, hoo, hoo, hooo, hooo, hoo that! AAAAAAAA, ha, ha, ha, ha, ha, ha, ha!!!" was Timmy's tortured response.

"Well then, it would appear you need some more persuasion Timmy. And I'm just the one who will enjoy persuading you," Chad chuckled at Timmy's predicament as he decided to up the ante on his boss man.

With that, Chad began plucking at Timmy's belt…

Timmy was so preoccupied with the tickling and hanging onto his chair that he was in no position to resist Chad soon had Timmy's belt unfastened and pulled it from his belt loops... Chad kept one hand working on Timmy's soles, not relinquishing any control he had gained over his boss. He picked up Timmy's letter opener and stabbed several holes in his boss' belt, about eight to twelve inches from the buckle. Then, he slipped the belt under Timmy's ankles, rebuckling the belt and using the new holes to create a leather restraint around Timmy's naked ankles. All the while Chad kept at least one hand working up and down Timmy's big smooth soles.

Next, Chad used his cell phone to snap a few pictures of his cackling screaming boss, to use as later ammunition. With the belt gone from Timmy's pants Chad easily managed to unfasten Timmy's slacks and pull down the zipper. When the fly opened Timmy's nine inches of enflamed maleness sprang out of his slacks...unfettered by any underpants. Chad giggled even more as he pulled on his boss man's slacks, lowering them as far as Timmy's knees, which was about as far as they would go, because he was sitting on Timmy's calves.

"CHAAAAADDDD, whaaaaaaat, ha, ha, ha, ha, ha, ha, haa WHATTTTT the fuuuuccckkkk are you dooooooooooing, ha, ha, ha, ha, ha to me hee, hee, hee, hee," Timmy wailed.

With one hand still scribbling on Timmy's soles Chad took more photos with his cell phone. Timmy looked so ridiculous, naked down to the knees and still in his dress shirt and tie. Then, Chad put his phone down and reached for Timmy's bouncing manhood. He squeezed, stroked and then worked an educated thumb right under the head of Timmy's raging erection. While still laughing his head off, Timmy's face registered shock, panic and lust all at once.

"OOOOOOO waaaaaaaaaa hee, hee, hee, hee, nooooo OH OOOOOOOOOOO, ha, ha, ha, ha, ha, ha!!!!" Timmy wailed, for he was now a mess.

Then, Chad stood up. Timmy was too tickled and weak from his raucous laughter to respond to the release of his legs that had been pinned to his desk. Chad quickly stripped Timmy's tie from his collar and ripped open his boss man's dress shirt.

(Well, Stephanie would now have to know about her handsome husband's latest adventure, since his ripped up shirt would be evidence.) Chad gave Timmy's ribs a quick tickling, sending his tortured boss into yet another fit of laughter. This latest tickling brought Timmy's hands together as he tried to protect his ribs. But Chad used this opportunity to quickly loop Timmy's tie around his wrists and tie it into a tight knot.

"OH NO, NO, NO Chad please, don't tie me up like this man," Timmy pleaded, laughing in between his rants. "OOOOOOOOO NOOOOOOO…"

Chad pulled Timmy onto the floor and using the boss man's own tie he secured Timmy's wrists to one of the huge feet on his desk. As Timmy squirmed in the bondage chad then tugged at his boss' suit pants, pulling them inside out and stretching Timmy's body so his arms were now pulled over his head. Timmy's suit pants could not come off because of the belt securing his ankles so Chad pulled them around and under the leg of the big couch in Timmy's office and tied them into a knot. Timmy was now totally stretched out, virtually naked between his desk and his couch.

Chad's actions had allowed Timmy to partially catch his breath.

"CHAD, stop this insanity…stop this now…" Timmy choked out weakly.

Chad grinned at Timmy and said, "Not until you have agreed to give me that raise!"

Timmy looked at Chad with panic in his eyes.

"CHAD, you know very well I can't promote a raise for you at this time of year, it's…it's just not done. It violates…EEEEEEEEE, hee, hee, hee, hee!!!!" Timmy began but could not finish his statement as Chad then dug his fingertips into his boss' armpits.

Timmy was helplessly tied between his own desk and the large leather couch. His own suit pants had been used to secure his ankles to the couch and his own tie and Chad's belt were securing his wrists to the leg of his desk. AND…Timmy was naked and vulnerable from his wrists to his ankles. His big man meat was hard as steel from all the tickling and Chad was now driving him insane with some more tickling…and poor Timmy was laughing his fool head off, screaming and cackling like, "EEEEEEEEEEEEEEE, hee, hee, hee, hee, heeeeeeeeeeeee!!!!!"

"OOOOOOOOOOOOO…hoo, hoo, hoo, EEEEEEEEEEEEE, hee, hee, hee, you bastard Chad!!!!" Timmy spat crazily.

Timmy shook his head from side to side and his muscular body vibrated and convulsed on the floor.

"IIIIIIEEEEEEEE give!!! HEE, HEE, HEE, HEE, HEEEEEEE!!! PLEEEAAASE, OOOOOOOOO ho, nooooo, ho, ho, ho, ho, ho, ho no moooorrrreeee ho, ho, ho, K, GIIIIEEEEEEEE hee, hee, hee, Riiiiiiiiizzzzzeeeee!!! Yuuuuuuuuuuuu, hoo, hoo, hoo, caaaaaaaaa ha, ha, ha, ha, ha, ha, ha haaaavvvve it!!!!!" Timmy screamed and finally caved to the horrible tickling that Chad was doing to his armpits.

Chad stopped his tickle torture and asked, "Timmy, are you saying that you are going to give me that raise that I want?"

Still chuckling, even though he was no longer being tickled, Timmy breathlessly but violently nodded his yes in the affirmative and whispered, "Yeeeeesss! You win. Now please turn me loose."

Chad grinned down at Timmy's virtually naked body stretched out before him, glistening real sexily with perspiration while he was still completely dressed. This gave the appearance of a switch in superiority roles…although Timmy was officially Chad's boss…it was Chad who was in charge now.

"I think I need for you to send an e-mail to HR, payroll, AND to the president of the bank, informing them of the raise you are granting me, Timmy," Chad said.

Timmy quickly replied, "Yes, yes, whatever…I'll do it. Just turn me loose."

Chad stood up and got Timmy's laptop. He sat back down in a chair near Timmy's middle. He pulled off his shoes and socks and rested one bare sexy foot on Timmy's chest and the other bare foot right beside Timmy's still hard and bobbing cock. Then Chad said, "Okay Timmy, hee, hee, my boss, I want you to dictate an e-mail to HR, payroll and the bank president, informing them of the raise that YOU are giving me…"

Timmy shook his head, "No Chad, I'll see that you giiiiiieeeeettt, OOOOOOOOOO UM, OOOOOO GOD!!!" Timmy suddenly screamed.

Chad saw Timmy's negative reaction and immediately began tweaking Timmy's very pronounced nipples with his bare toes…and at the same time Chad used his other foot to jostle Timmy's ball sac and stroke his hard throbbing cock. Chad stroked Timmy's enflamed cock with his bare foot and diddled the surface with his wiggling toes… Then, Chad slipped his other foot from Timmy's nipples to his boss man's exposed armpit and dug his toes into the hairy region…

"AAAAAAAAAAAAAA hahahahahahahahahahahahahaha… noooooooo OOOOOOOK pleeeeeeeeeaaaase Stoooooooooop hee, hee, hee, hee, hee, hee…" Timmy screeched.

Timmy immediately gave in and dictated a memo to HR, Payroll and the bank president that even though it was not in line with bank personnel policy, he was making an exception and granting Chad Wilkins a mid-year raise…effective immediately.

"Okay, that is great!" Chad said to Timmy. "Now I need your password to send this forward.

Chad looked questioningly at his near naked boss' stretched out feet. Timmy hesitated and Chad's toes simply flinched in his boss' exposed armpit. Timmy wiggled and blurted out, "ticklingchinaman!"

"Ah, ha, ha, your password is ticklingchinaman? Holy fuck boss…I really think that underneath all that helpless laughter you really are a pervert," Chad laughingly replied as he entered the password and hit Enter.

Timmy simply blushed and made no comment.

"Thank you boss, I will make you proud and pleased that you gave me this raise, even if it was a little, ha, ha, ticklish for you to do," Chad chuckled. "Now, there is just one more little item that I need for you to agree to."

As he spoke Chad grinned devilishly at Timmy.

"And I just know you are going to agree to comply with my wishes here too!" Chad said.

"What now?" Timmy crossly responded. "You have brazenly tickle stripped me and coerced a raise out of me, which is completely against bank policy. Now what could you possibly want...my job???"

"Ha, ha...noooooo Timmy, I don't want your job, you are too good at what you do and too valuable to the bank," Chad laughed. "No, what I want is a favor...just a little favor..."

This time as Chad spoke his right foot continued to stroke Timmy's hard as steel cock.

"God, what then?" Timmy asked miserably. "And please leave my penis alone, God stop that, OOOOOOOOOOOO stop please."

Timmy was reluctantly very sexily stimulated.

"Timmy, Sir, your secretary is leaving to have and raise a baby, so, with that in mind, you need to replace her and my cousin, Bobby Wilkins needs that job," Chad said and looked questioningly at Timmy, while his left sided toes very gently stroked his boss man's armpit.

Timmy twisted in his bound naked state and said, "What? What are you asking me to do? I already have a candidate for that position... OOOOOO, hee, hee, hee, oh no, no, please don't start that infernal tickling again Chad...hee, hee, please."

Obviously Chad was being very persuasive.

"Great! Bobby will be so pleased and proud to work for you; he really is a good administrative assistant. AND because he is gay, he really won't be a sexual distraction to you like all the other legs around here are," Chad laughed.

"GAY? He's gay?" Timmy questioned.

"Yes Sir, so like I said, he won't be a sexual distraction for you. But then, he does like the challenge of a straight guy, especially one as handsome and studly as you are Timmy," Chad said with humor.

"God, how can this kind of stuff happen to me???" Timmy said out loud, but really more to himself.

"Now, I know you are an honorable man, but these pictures in my cell phone will insure that you follow through with hiring Bobby. I will release you now Timmy. Although I really would like to satisfy that big leaking cock of yours, but sadly, I don't have the time. You see, I have somewhere to be and I really do appreciate you being so cooperative with me here tonight," Chad said, pulled his socks and shoes back on and then released Timmy from his bonds.

"Good night boss," Chad said as he hurried out of Timmy's office with a huge grin on his face.

Timmy simply sat there on his Persian rug, his arms locked around his knees, virtually naked with his suit pants and dress shirt a mass of sweaty wrinkles. His cock was still leaking from his sexual excitement from being tickled and he thought he would just go home to his sexy wife Stephanie and get the relief he desperately needed. That's it… he would go home and make passionate love to Stephanie and deal with this raise and hiring a gay secretary later.

When Timmy got home to his sexy wife, Stephanie, his cock was still hard from the intense tickling he had endured from Chad.

He figured that coming home rock hard in his suit pants he would make passionate and mad man love to his wife. Stephanie greeted Timmy at the door and looked at his totally wrinkled and soiled suit and giggled.

"Timmy, oh my, Timmy!" Stephanie sighed. "Have you met yet another tickle dominant?"

Now it was Timmy's turn to sigh, gathered Stephanie into his muscular arms, and his tented slacks poked her abdomen.

"Yes dear!" Timmy honestly explained. "That damned assistant of mine, Chad, he had hung around the office until he and I were the only ones left there. Then he proceeded to tickle the shit out of me and even used my own clothes to bind me the fuck up. I swear, I was powerless against the fucking guy."

Stephanie laughed and asked, "Whatever did he do that for?" Timmy sighed again and told his wife about the raise that Chad had tickled out of him and the gay cousin he'd have to hire as his new secretary. Stephanie simply laughed again, but Timmy said, "Come on, let's go to bed...I want to make love to you. I have a raging hard-on in my suit pants that won't quit."

This time Stephanie laughed her sexy laugh and said, "Honey, that would be so nice, but, Valerie and Douglas are coming for a late supper. Then, the doorbell rang and Stephanie exclaimed, "Oh that must be them now."

"No!" Timmy pleaded.

"Yes honey and I want you to be very nice..." Stephanie said and tugged at her handsome husband's tie. "But you look terrible..."

And so, the evening progressed where poor Timmy yet again wound up naked and this time at the mercy of Valerie's gay assistant, Douglas...and Stephanie extended her lesbian encounter with Valerie... right under Timmy's nose...

Well, not really because Timmy was once again a bit tied up and distracted, and laughing, "HA, HA, HA, HA, HA, HA, HA, "

But once again that is a story for another time...

Rafael

Author: Christopher Trevor

"Ohhhhhh man," I groaned miserably as I woke up, still tied in a spread-eagle position to the bed in Albert's guestroom. "Shit, that fucker left me tied up like this all night. I can't believe I actually slept like this."

It was Sunday morning. I looked over at the digital clock on the night table and saw that it was eight AM. I squirmed on the bed, trying hopelessly to get myself untied, but it was useless. Albert had tied me tighter than a drum and I wasn't going anywhere anytime soon. I was wearing just my white (piss and sweat soaked) Calvin Klein briefs and a pair of smelly silk beige colored Perry Ellis calf-length dress socks. My socks were drenched and stinking with saliva from Albert and his buddies having licked my damned feet the night before. Fuck, can you believe that shit? A bunch of dudes licked my damned feet while I was wearing my socks, of all things huh? Yeah, but I sure as hell smelled like a fucking locker room and I guessed that that was why Albert had stashed me away in his guestroom for the night. After Albert's buddies had gone home the night before I really wasn't all that surprised when Albert decided he would keep me in his guestroom overnight. I mean, I was already all tied up and totally powerless to stop him after all. Then, as I laid there squirming on the bed Albert came into the room. Smiling, wearing only his underpants, he sauntered over to me and knelt at one of my smelly feet.

"Good morning Rafael," he said to me mockingly.

"Yeah, good morning," I replied sarcastically as Albert placed his fingers around my foot.

"Did you sleep well?" he asked me and squeezed my foot, sniffing at my moist and raunchy sock.

"As well as can be expected, given the position I'm in," I responded, trying to sound angry. "I just can't believe you left me tied up like this all night.

"You were never in any danger of losing blood circulation," Albert said, leaned down and pressed his nose and mouth against one of my bound feet. "The way I tied you last night was tight enough so that you wouldn't be able to free yourself, but, still loose enough so you wouldn't have any circulation issues."

"Thanks, I guess," I said with a grin. "I feel like I've been kidnapped by one of my best friends."

"That's because in a way you have been kidnapped," Albert responded. "…by one of your very best friends."

Albert stuck his tongue out and trailed it up and down the bottom of my foot, tickling me.

"Oh God no," I half whimpered and half laughed. "Didn't you and your two buddies work me over enough last night?"

"Sure," Albert replied. "But now Mike and Ronnie are gone and I have you all to myself. That's why I tied you up in here last night."

Albert proceeded to lick my foot harder, tickling me even more.

"Speaking of my being tied up, when the hell are you going to untie me?" I asked anxiously.

"Not for a while," Albert said mischievously and gave one of my sock covered toes a hard suck, sending chills through me. "Not for quite a while. You really got yourself into a really fucked up situation last night when you agreed to the rules of the game Rafael."

As Albert licked and tickled my foot my cock grew piss hard in my stinking briefs and I knew I would have to piss in them. Albert and his two buddies had had a great fucking time the night before tickling the tar out of me and forcing me to piss in my damned briefs. I squirmed more miserably on the bed, begging Albert to stop tickling me, and remembering how I had gotten myself into this mess in the first place the night before.

It was Saturday night and my co-worker Albert (a cute Columbian guy with black hair and a thick mustache) had invited me and two of our other co-workers to his apartment for an old fashioned and friendly game of Go Fish and beer and pretzels. (I just didn't realize how friendly the game would become until I agreed to the rules while we were playing.) Not having any other plans I accepted Albert's offer. When I arrived Mike (a tall, very muscular Irish guy) and Ronnie (a short and portly guy) were already there.

"Hey, you're late!" Ronnie yelled jokingly as Albert ushered me into the apartment. "There's no beer or pretzels left for you."

"Yeah, you probably ate them all," I replied in my El Salvadorian accent.

Mike and Albert laughed at my comment, I handed Albert the two cold six-packs I had brought along, and I sat down at the card table with the other guys.

Albert refilled the pretzel bowl, placed a few of the cold beers from my six packs on the table, placed the rest of them in the refrigerator, and dealt out the cards. That was when the trouble started. Halfway through the game I saw that I was winning and I suppose that the two beers I had already drunk were making me mouthy. I was thoroughly convinced that I was going to win.

"Shit, we should have played for money," I said, opening my third beer and taking a long hearty chug of it. "I'm going to win this fucking game easily."

"Don't be so fucking sure Raffy," Mike said. "It ain't over till it's over."

"Man, if we were playing for money I would be cleaning you guys out right now," I stated mockingly.

"What if we were playing *for something?*" Albert asked, glaring at me angrily.

"Like what?" I asked.

"Like the loser has to do anything the winners say," Albert said threateningly. "The loser being the first sap to lose all his cards of course."

I instantly (and stupidly) agreed to that and so did Mike and Ronnie. I knew that the first thing I would make Mike do when I had won was to take his shirt off. For such a long time I had wanted to see his big chest and feast on his big manly tits that always poked so provocatively against any shirt he wore.

I was planning to make Mike stand with his hands behind himself as I feasted heartily and slowly and methodically on those tits of his. Albert looked at me, smirked, and said, "Let's get on with the game. Give me all your king cards."

That came as a surprise because I didn't know that Albert was holding a king card. I handed over my three kings and felt a small shiver of nervousness course through me. A few minutes later the tables had been turned and I found I was losing the game, most miserably at that.

Albert opened a fourth beer for me and slid it over to where I was seated.

"I have to go and piss," I said, starting to stand up.

"Sit down," Albert said harshly. "No pissing till the game is over."

"I haven't lost yet!" I said loudly. "And I have to piss real fucking bad."

"Relax, it'll be over soon," Albert said to me with a wicked looking smile on his face. "Then you'll piss, in the meantime, drink up!"

Albert reached across the table, handed me my fourth beer and I took a long chug from it.

"Looks like you have something special in mind for the loser of the game Albert," Mike said, looking at me.

"Oh I sure do Mike," Albert said longingly. "I sure as shit do."

I gulped more beer and felt my pride slipping away. I was down to four damned cards and I didn't stand a snowball's chance in hell. And man, but I had to piss. A few more minutes went by and then the game was over. I had lost. Fuck, I was the first guy to lose all his damned cards. Albert wound up with the most cards, followed by Mike, and Ronnie came in third.

"Okay Albert, I lose," I said, sounding totally defeated. "Can I go and piss now?"

No," Albert said loudly. "But you can strip your clothes off down to your socks and underpants."

"What???" I asked in disbelief. "Now look, when I agreed that the loser would have to do anything the winners said I had no fucking idea you had this in mind."

"Stripping you is just the beginning," Albert said tauntingly. "After that we're going to tie you the fuck up."

"Hey, now this sounds like real fucking fun!" Mike said happily and clapped his big hands together. "Where's the rope Albert?"

Albert smiled and pointed to the kitchen.

"In the cabinet under the sink," Albert said to Mike, looking at me fiendishly. "Would you please go and get it Mike?"

Mike stood up and dashed to the kitchen, laughing as he went.

"Ha, ha, ha, I cannot believe we're going to strip that sexy El Salvadorian guy and rope him the fuck up," Mike cackled gleefully in the kitchen.

I looked at Albert helplessly.

"You have got to be joking," I whispered desperately. "Right?"

"Ronnie lets you and I help Rafael to get undressed," Albert said to his portly buddy.

They stood up, came over to me, and hauled me roughly to my feet by my upper arms.

"Now wait just a damned minute here!" I shouted as Albert began unbuttoning my red and black flannel shirt.

In what seemed like seconds my shirt was off me, exposing my smooth and hairless and somewhat muscular chest. Ronnie helped Albert to undo the fastener on my pants as Mike came back with mounds upon mounds of rope. Mike did the honors of quickly roping my wrists behind me as my beige shoes were taken off my feet.

Moments later I stood before the three men, my so-called work buddies, in just my white Calvin Klein briefs and beige Perry Ellis socks. Albert ran his hands over my chest as Ronnie and Mike busied themselves tying my feet, my thighs and my knees. They ran their big mangy hands over my sexy legs, snapped the elastic in my socks and underpants and teased me mercilessly by gently running their fingers over my piss hard cock and my balls, which were aching in my damned briefs.

"Fuckers!" I yelled angrily. "The very least you can do is let me piss."

"Who's stopping you?" Albert teased me. "Go ahead, piss."

"In my briefs???" I asked him in shock.

Albert hooked a hand around my arm and squeezed it hard.

"You really don't have much of a choice my loud mouthed friend," Albert said softly and directly into my ear, his tongue just grazing it. "We're not taking you to the bathroom any time soon."

With that Albert tied a blindfold over my eyes and then roped my arms tightly at the elbows.

"Shit, blindfolding me too eh you fucker?" I panted.

"Ronnie, shuffle the cards," Albert said. "We'll play another game."

"What about me???" I blurted loudly.

"You?" Albert asked, squeezing my small, brown and pointy nipples. "You're going to stand here balanced on your cute bound up feet while we play cards. When we're done, if you still haven't pissed I'll find a way to make you piss."

"Shit," I seethed. "What a fucked up thing to do to a guy you call your buddy."

What a mess I had gotten myself into. The four beers I had consumed were really taking their evil toll. I was slightly drunk and every second that passed I had to piss more and more. My cock ached long and hard in my briefs. The guys sat there playing cards, virtually ignoring me. (But then, just how easy is it to ignore the fact that one of your buddies is standing nearby stripped, tied up, and blindfolded?) Albert had told me that if I complained or demanded to be untied he would gag me, with one of portly Ronnie's socks. With that in mind you know I kept my big mouth shut. When they finished their card game I still hadn't pissed. I was sweating and I rocked on my bound feet in utter agony as I heard the guys announce that they had to piss and one at a time went to the bathroom. Albert sidled up next to me at one point and forced me to gulp down some ice water. He then rubbed some of the ice water on my nipples and spilled some of it on my briefs.

"Albert, *please,"* I whimpered. "I-I just can't hold it anymore!"

Albert laughed and said, "Hey guys, watch this!" Then, I felt Albert's fingertips moving slowly over my bare stomach area and sides, tickling me, holy SHIT!

"Ha, ha," I sputtered. "Hey, that fucking tickles!"

As the words left my mouth I realized what a huge mistake I had made. Albert tickled me more and then I knew that I was going to piss into my briefs.

"Albert, please man, this is mortifying!" I yelled.

I gyrated my lean yet slightly muscular body and then it happened. I pissed long and hard into my white briefs.

"Whoooooo!!!" Ronnie whooped. "Fuckin' way to go Raffy boy! Soak those briefs of yours! Get 'em smelling real nice and pissy."

I felt Ronnie's and Mike's big hands moving over me also as Albert continued tickling me on my stomach and sides. When I stopped pissing my briefs were indeed soaked in the front and I smelled the rancid yellow liquid.

"Okay, I pissed!" I yelled angrily and miserably. "Would you fuckers please untie me now??? And for God's sake, stop tickling me!!"

But Albert said it would be a long fucking time before I was untied. Besides, he and Ronnie and Mike were now ready for yet another game of cards. I would again remain standing, tied, and having to piss again real soon. Big muscular Mike lifted me off the floor and stood me next to the card table where he was sitting. (Mike, fucking muscle guy with the great tits that I had planned on chewing on after I had won the game…shit…)

As all three of my buddies played cards I felt Mike's hand toying with my legs and my bubble butt. Now my cock was filling up not just with piss, but a good sized load of El Salvadorian creamy cum also. The damned card game went slowly and I pissed again into my briefs, grunting and groaning as Albert and Ronnie laughed hysterically and Mike continued running his hand over my legs and butt cheeks.

"How does he feel?" Ronnie asked Mike.

"He feels good," Mike replied, placing his hand on the front of my wet briefs. "And wet, he feels wet."

The three men laughed and then later finished their third game of cards. Albert suggested that they work on me some more. I dreaded to think what I was in for next.

A few moments later I was stretched out atop the card table on my back. What a sight I was let me tell you. Albert was again tickling my stomach and sides, this time with a goose feather. Mike and Ronnie were squatting at my feet and licking them hard, tickling me even more. I laughed, cried, and shook uncontrollably on the table. I begged my three buddies to stop but they were relentless, tickling me more and more. I pissed some more into my briefs and my cock remained super hard and aching, filled with a good sized load of manly cum.

Next, my buddies flipped me over onto my stomach. Albert did the honors of pulling my briefs down in the back and ran the feather over my smooth butt cheeks and in my ass crack as Mike and Ronnie tortured my armpits with their fingertips, poking and tickling them hard.

"God, this is too fucking much guys!!!" I screamed. "P-please, stop it already!!"

But the night was young and the torture had just begun. After they were done tickling me I was sweating from head to toe. Albert gave me a cold drink of water and then he told Mike and Ronnie that it was time to spank me. *Shit!!!*

Moments passed and I found myself next standing in the center of the room, still tied but no longer blindfolded. My briefs were thoroughly soaked with piss and sweat and still pulled down in the back. Albert, Ronnie and Mike were all sitting at the card table, each holding a leather paddle in their hands. Looking at them I gulped hard and asked, "Okay, so I'm going to be spanked, probably real fucking hard too. Which one of you fuckers gets to go first? Albert smiled fiendishly and gestured for me to go over to him. I looked down at my tied feet and looked at Albert in disbelief. He simply gestured again for me to go over to him. I huffed miserably and then hopped on my bound feet over to my buddy. He laid me across his knees and ran his hand over my firm, round, bubble butt cheeks.

"Nice ass Raffy," Albert said lustfully. "Real nice…"

With that, he brought the paddle he was holding down on my butt, hard. I yelped in pain as he whacked my ass over and over and harder and harder with each blow.

"OWWWWWWW!!!" I roared. "C'mon Albert, give me a break already!! YOWWWWW!!! Let's not lose sight of the fact that we're all buddies here! OWWWWWW!!!"

After twenty hard whacks my butt cheeks were crimson but Albert still continued the paddling.

"Albert, *please stop!!*" I begged through clenched teeth.

After ten more hard whacks Albert finally stopped.

He pulled me to my feet in front of him and I stood there crying in pain as he pulled my piss smelling hard cock out of my soaked and rancid briefs.

"WH-what now???" I asked breathlessly as Albert held my throbbing cock in his fist.

Without a word Albert leaned forward, slurped my hard cock into his mouth, and began vigorously sucking it.

"OHHHHH yeah," I crooned.

I swiveled my hips and rocked on my bound feet as Albert sucked me harder and harder. He teased my piss hole with the tip of his tongue and I swiveled my body more, doing what looked like a dance of utter ecstasy.

"Oh fuck yeah; I'm going to shoot my fucking creamy load!" I announced breathlessly.

Albert took my cock out of his mouth, pulled my briefs back up and over it, and I shot my big pent-up load into them.

"OH GOD, yeah, yeah!! Feel so good to do this in my damned briefs!" I bellowed as I stood there shooting my load.

When I was done I pissed again into my briefs.

"Hey Raffy, get over here and get your next paddling!" Mike said, holding up his leather paddle. "We don't want you feeling good all that long now."

I looked at Albert beseechingly.

"Albert, please, no more man," I begged. "Please man, my butt can't take this!"

Albert smiled and gestured for me to go over to Mike. Whimpering, I hopped my way over to Mike, (looking at those tits of his poking against his shirt. God, how I wanted those tits of his…) laid down across his knees and he ran his hand over my red butt. Then, he brought the paddle down on it, hard. I began screaming in pain again. Mike paddled my butt relentlessly, just as Albert had. I was by now crying profusely and begging Mike to stop. My poor butt felt like there were welts on it. I looked up at one point and saw Ronnie waiting his turn to paddle me. Fuck, what a night it had turned out to be. And I was in this mess only because of my damned big mouth.

After twenty to thirty whacks to my ass Mike stopped paddling me. Like Albert, he stood me in front of himself on my bound feet. Tears soaked my face as Mike extracted my cock from my briefs, toyed with it for a few moments, and then greedily gobbled it into his mouth.

"Coming up, gusher number two!" Albert teased me from his seat. "Ready to shoot another load Raffy boy?"

I rocked in a man's passion as Mike sucked my rod. And I was hard again in seconds.

Looking over at Albert in disbelief over all that had transpired thus far this night I simply moaned, "OOO yeah…yeah man…"

"Hurry up and cum Rafael!" Ronnie shouted then. "I want my damned turn at paddling you!"

"Bastard," I seethed through clenched teeth.

Mike grabbed my fire engine red butt cheeks in his big hands and pulled my cock further into his mouth with each suck and gobble. I was by then swooning and sweating in a mixture of pain and ecstasy.

"OH GOD," I panted breathlessly.

A few moments later I did indeed shoot my second load, right into Mike's mouth.

The big muscular guy with the great tits gulped down my El Salvadorian jazz, forcefully sucking every possible drop out of my cock hole. FUCK, even after I had stopped cumming Mike kept his lips wrapped tightly around the tip of my manhood, teasing the fuck out of it with the tip of his tongue, causing chills to consume me. He sucked me some more, causing me erotic pain.

"OHHHHHH GOD, I should piss in your mouth you fucker!" I snarled.

"Uh-oh, he's going to get paddled extra hard for that remark," Ronnie said anxiously.

I looked over at Ronnie and loudly called him a bastard. He only laughed at me and wiggled his tongue suggestively at my butt. Mike finally released my cock from his mouth and let go of my butt cheeks. He packed my cock back into my briefs as I stood there catching my breath.

"I've seen you looking at my chest all night Raffy boy," Mike said and rolled his shirt up, revealing his big, pointy, and fleshy tits that I adored so much.

I looked down at Mike's tits with my tongue practically hanging out of my mouth.

"Go ahead Raffy boy, take a suck or a few of my big tits," Mike said, running a hand over his chest most seductively. "It'll give you some extra time before you're paddled by Ronnie."

The three men laughed as I hopped to Mike's side, leaned over as best I could on my bound feet, and heartily slurped one of the guy's big tits into my mouth.

"OHHHHH yeah, that feels great Raffy boy," Mike crooned and ran his hand through my silky black straight hair.

Ronnie waited for me to hop over to him as I sucked, slurped, and kissed one of Mike's tits. Fuck, I was in ecstasy, at least I had gotten to suck one of Mike's tits, a dream come true for me.

"C'mon Rafael, come and get it!" Ronnie ordered. "I'm waiting for you, and so is my paddle."

I stopped sucking Mike's tit, stood up straight, looked at Albert, and my eyes filled with tears.

"Albert please, enough of this already huh?" I pleaded. "I am in such horrible pain! Please man, untie me already!"

Albert came over to me, stepped behind me, and placed his hands on my upper arms.

"We're far from done with you pal of mine," he said softly. "Now, hop on over to Ronnie and get spanked before I decide that we're all going to have a second go each at that hot ass of yours!"

Albert let go of my arms and gave my ass a hard slap with the back of his hand to get me moving. I instantly hopped over to Ronnie amid the laughing and cackling of my three buddies. I laid myself across the portly man's knees and without waiting a second he began paddling me, hard, real fucking hard.

"ARRRGHHHH!!!" I screamed in agony and thrashed on Ronnie's knees.

"Give him a few good ones for threatening to piss in my mouth Ronnie," Mike said and Ronnie did just that.

He paddled my ass till it shone more than bright red. All I heard after a while was myself screaming in utter agony as Ronnie must have given me at least thirty five hard spanks with his leather paddle.

"Enough!" Albert suddenly said loudly and Ronnie stopped paddling me. "Suck him off."

Ronnie yanked me to my feet and I stood in front of him crying, sweating profusely, and shaking uncontrollably. Albert came up behind me and placed a hand on the back of my neck.

"Easy buddy, easy," Albert whispered in my ear as Ronnie took my cock out of my rancid briefs and into his mouth.

I gasped as Ronnie sucked me toward gusher number three, and as he did so Albert pulled my briefs up in the back. I managed to calm down as I was again taken to ecstasy as Ronnie sucked me gently and passionately. It took a while longer for me to shoot a third load, but fuck, I did, I fucking did. Ronnie let me shoot my juices into my briefs and then stroked me till I pissed into them again as well. Man, but my briefs smelled heavy duty of piss, cum, and sweat. If a guy's briefs ever told a story, mine sure did at that moment. Albert helped me over to my chair and sat me down.

"Feeling okay?" he asked me.

"Y-yes," I replied. "Can I maybe have a cold drink though?"

Albert placed a bottle of cold beer to my lips and I gulped it down. He stroked my hair as I drank the beer.

"Will you untie me now?" I asked him hopefully.

"Untie you? Untie you buddy?" Albert asked. "But Rafael, we haven't cum yet."

I looked at the three men and they were all taking their cocks out of their jeans at the same moment. Mike's shirt was still rolled up, revealing his tits.

"Seeing as I paddled you the hardest I get to go first," Ronnie said. "Get the fuck over here and get on your knees loudmouth!"

Well, sucking cock would sure as hell be better than being tickled and having the shit paddled out of me. I pulled myself to my feet and hopped over to Ronnie. I knelt down in front of the guy and slurped his soft cock into my mouth. As I sucked him his cock grew stiff in my craw.

"This sure is a hell of a good way to keep his big yap shut," Ronnie said, holding me by the back of my neck and stroking my hair. "God almighty, this feels great though! OHHHHHH fuck…"

As I sucked Ronnie's cock Albert stepped behind me and tied the blindfold back over my eyes.

"Oh yeah, suck me boy, suck my hard cock!" Ronnie moaned.

I pushed my tongue into his big piss hole and swirled it around in there a little. Ronnie moaned louder in a man's passion.

"OHHHH GAWD, I'm getting close already man!" Ronnie announced breathlessly. "Stand the fuck back you little shit!!"

I did as I was told and Ronnie grabbed his cock. He shot his load all over my briefs, adding to the mess that was already in them, now the mess would be on the outside.

"OH yeah!! Yeah!" Ronnie grunted loudly as he spewed his load on my briefs.

Next, he grabbed the front of my briefs, pulled them forward, stood up, and pissed long and hard into them, all over my soft cock, my balls and my dark nest of sexy pubic hair. I clenched my teeth in anger as Ronnie pissed long, hard, hot and yellow into my already rancid scented briefs.

"Fucker!!" I ranted angrily. *"Pissing all over me!!"*

The fucking guy's piss dripped down my legs and then he let go of my briefs, letting the elastic waistband snap back against my skin.

"I'm next!" I heard Mike say anxiously.

Mike positioned me in front of him on my knees and slipped his already hard huge Irish cock into my mouth. God, it felt so big that I thought it would literally tear my mouth apart as he forced it in. He pumped my mouth slowly, oozing pre cum out of his dick hole. I licked, sucked, and even kissed Mike's big throbbing hard-on. Actually, of all the three men Mike had the biggest, fattest, and longest cock so I really didn't mind sucking him off. Not to mention that the handsome bastard had met me slurp on one of his colossal tits.

"Oh yeah, suck my meat stick you little bastard!" Mike said breathlessly, caressing the back of my neck and stroking my soft and silky hair.

A few minutes later Mike shot his bug creamy Irish load, right into my mouth. I managed to swallow most of it, the rest of it dripped down my chin and landed on my chest. That looked real sexy. Mike grunted loudly as his throbbing cock spewed gushes upon gushes of creamy Irish jazz into my mouth. When he was done Mike let his cock slip out of my mouth, (I licked his stray cum off my lips) he pulled me to my feet, and I felt all three of the men running their hands over me, touching and squeezing me everywhere, licking and slurping the stray cum off my chest, really slurping hard at my nipples, and pinching and twisting my nubs too.

"OHHHHH you fuckers," I moaned helplessly yet contentedly.

Later, with my blindfold off I found myself stretched out on the table again on my back with my feet untied. Mike and Ronnie were each holding one of my beige socked feet in their hands and licking them feverishly, tickling me like crazy at the same fucking time. Albert leaned over me, played with my nipples, and stifled my laughter by kissing me hard over and over on the lips.

"Oh man, his feet sure do stink!" Ronnie said as he knelt there lapping at my socked toes.

"Yeah, they sure do, but I can't get enough of them!" Mike said.

"Please stop," I began, but Albert clamped his mouth down on mine, silencing me again. "MMMFFFF…"

Albert kissed me long and hard, pushing his tongue deep into my mouth.

"Mmmm…" I crooned.

Albert stopped kissing me, gently stroked my hair, and looked adoringly into my eyes.

"God almighty, you're beautiful," Albert whispered.

This time when he kissed me I responded passionately. Mike and Ronnie continued licking my feet and my cock grew hard in my soaked and stinking briefs.

Later, at the door Albert said good-night to Mike and Ronnie. I watched from the table, still stretched out on my back and tied the fuck up.

Mike and Ronnie thanked Albert for a great and most interesting evening and kissed him good-night.

"What are you going to do with him?" Ronnie asked Albert, pointing at me.

"Oh, I think I'll keep him here for the night," Albert replied fiendishly. "He's really in no condition to go home."

The two men thanked Albert one more time and left. Albert locked the door and slowly walked over to me.

"Now, what am I going to do with you Rafael?" Albert asked me with a grin.

I watched as he knelt down and started licking my stinking socked feet.

A while later Albert carried me over his shoulder like a sack of potatoes to the guest bedroom where he proceeded to tie me to the bed in a spread-eagle position. He told me to sleep well, wished me a good night, and told me that if I needed to piss that I should just piss into my briefs, again.

As the memories of the night before faded Albert *finally* untied me. I sat up on the bed with him holding my socked feet in his hands.

"You can take a shower if you want to," Albert said good naturedly. "I'll make us some coffee and breakfast."

"Okay," I replied.

"How does your ass feel?" he asked me, sounding like he felt a little sorry for me and what I had gone through.

Smiling, I said that it felt sore but that I would survive. Albert rolled my beige socks off my feet and held them tightly in his hand.

"I want to keep these," Albert said, holding up my socks. "And your briefs too. I'll give you fresh briefs and socks for your trip home later."

I stood up, slipped my briefs off, and walked toward the door to the bedroom.

"Hey," Albert called out and I turned around, facing him. "You were a good sport last night, a real good sport."

I smiled and walked naked to the bathroom to shower. Albert sat on the bed sniffing my rancid briefs and socks, the pervert. I stayed for breakfast and coffee and then Albert suggested we play a game of cards, the loser having to do anything the winner wanted and said.

The Nightshift

Author: Christopher Trevor

My name is Ben. I've worked as a security director for a jewelry corporation for the last ten years or so and nothing as scary or exciting has ever happened before that compares to the story I'm about to tell you. As part of my job I have to fill in for the manager of the nightshift when he's out sick or on vacation. For the purposes of this story he was out sick. It was a Wednesday and he had called in sick at the last minute, which meant I had to work a double shift. I was dressed in olive colored trousers, a white button down shirt, a patterned silk necktie, black slip-on wingtips, and black calf-length cotton dress socks. I thought about how sweaty smelling I would be by two in the morning, seeing as I'd put on my clothes at six AM the morning before.

Ah well, such is life. I called my wife and told her not to wait up. I also told her that I would be ordering dinner in. At five thirty PM the dayshift filed out and the nightshift workers filed in.

(My office is a few feet from the entrance of the floor we're situated on.) What I'm now going to tell you about happened at approximately ten PM and went on till about twelve thirty AM (I think.) At nine forty I called the all night diner by my building and ordered a sandwich and soup for dinner. When it arrived fifteen minutes later one of the nightshift guys picked it up at the receiving window and brought it to my office. (Till this day I don't remember who brought the food in. I probably never even looked up at him as he set it down on my desk.)

I ate quickly and a few moments later it happened. I began feeling tired and dizzy at the same time. My vision blurred and I couldn't even stand up. I had enough time to realize that my food had been drugged as I passed out in my swivel chair.

I came to a while later to find myself tied to my swivel chair. I mean securely fucking tied. My arms were crossed behind me and bound to the metal rung on the chair, my waist was tied around the chair a few times, my thighs were tied down to the chair by mounds of rope, and my feet were tied in a crossed position to the swivel mechanism on the bottom of the chair. I was gagged with a rag stuffed in my mouth and a rope tied over it, jamming it firmly in place. My shoes were off my feet and had been placed in a corner by the wall; my necktie was pulled down a notch with my top shirt button opened. Most frightening of all though was the fact that the zipper on my pants was wide open and my cock and balls were hanging freely out of it.

Needless to say I panicked. I struggled like crazy to pull free but it was no use. The ropes were tied too damned tight. I didn't dare make a sound behind the gag for fear of being found this way. But someone had done this to me, so I more than likely had been seen. *But who???* I thought about it and realized that being the security director of the company I wasn't all that well-liked by the employees. Obviously someone had come up with a way to play a horrible joke on me.

Suddenly, my thoughts were cut off by my office door being slightly opened. A hand snaked its way in and flicked off the light switch on the wall by the door.

The light in the hallway was off also so when my office door opened all the way I could not see who came in or how many of them there were.

I made some "MMMMFFF" sounds and heard the sound of giggling. Then, a cloth was placed over my eyes and tied behind my head. Whoever was in my office had now added to my agony by blindfolding me. I heard more giggling. I figured there had to be three people in my office, all male, that was what my instincts told me. I then heard my office door close and the light switch flicked back on. I was spun around on the swivel chair a few times till I was dizzy as hell.

My chair stopped spinning and I heard a disguised voice say, "He's facing you, do it." I could not believe what happened next. A mouth closed around my exposed cock and began sucking it. I was in a state of total shock. Here I was, tied up, gagged, and blindfolded in my own damned office, having my cock sucked by an unseen male employee. I struggled angrily against the confining ropes as his tongue swirled around my hard cock. I felt his tongue teasing the shaft of my cock as well, and then it flicked into my piss hole, forcing it open. My struggles were fruitless and he sucked me harder and harder, leading me toward orgasm. I felt his hands roaming over my legs and down to my feet. I felt another pair of hands moving over my arms from behind me and squeezing my tits.

I was helpless, yet in a state of forced ecstasy. Then it happened. I came, I shot my load. Whoever was sucking my cock forced every drop of my cum into his mouth and swallowed it. I shook and trembled in the chair and sputtered like crazy behind the gag. Now that I'd cum I figured I would be untied and the joke would be over, but, no such luck.

When whoever he was, was done sucking me I heard him pull himself to his feet.

"Spin him again," he said in that disguised voice. "We'll see who goes next."

So, once again they spun me around in my swivel chair, and once again I was dizzied. When I stopped spinning this time I heard the disguised voice say, "It's your turn." I felt another mouth close around my softening cock and begin sucking it. I was forced toward a second erection amid the sounds of giggling. Once again I felt hands roaming over me, touching and squeezing my tits under my shirt, squeezing my feet, and caressing the back of my neck. The person sucking me moved his tongue down to my balls and gently lapped them. I have to admit that despite the situation it felt awesome!

Moments later he deep-throated my cock and I shot a second load, squirting it directly into the guy's gullet. I was sweating like crazy and by then saliva dripped from the sides of my gagged mouth. My cock slid out of the guy's mouth and I heard my second unseen sucker pull himself to his feet.

All three of the men in my office were giggling like girls it sounded like, but I knew that these were no girls. They were touching me all over while they giggled at my predicament, and rape.

"One more time," one of them whispered fiendishly in my ear. "And this time we're going to do you the hard way."

In moments I found out just what they meant by the hard way. My feet were untied from the swivel mechanism of the chair and my thighs were untied as well. I was pulled to my numb feet and felt my trousers being unbuttoned and pulled down. I was furious, but helpless to stop them as my arms were still bound tightly behind me, and I was still gagged and blindfolded.

Two of them held me balanced by my (bound) arms as the third one helped me out of my pants, followed by my briefs!

I was shocked, appalled, and erotically aroused all at the same time. I was guided back into my chair and my socked feet were placed up on the desk and retied. What a position I was in now. I felt one of the men crawl underneath my legs and pull my cock and balls down between my thighs. My thighs were then tied together as the man underneath me took my cock in his mouth, sucked it, and teased my dangling nuts with his fingertips. (I assumed the one sucking me now was the third guy in the room, taking his turn at me.) As my cock was being sucked for the third time in less than an hour I also felt mouths close around each of my socked feet. Each of the other two men held my bound feet and sucked my toes, through my thin dress socks no less. I could not believe the position I was in, balls ass naked with my feet up on my desk, having my cock sucked, my balls teased, and my damned smelly toes sucked all at once.

I "MMMFFED" like crazy behind the gag as my cock was savagely sucked to a third erection. I didn't think I had it in me to cum a third time in such a short span of time. (I learned otherwise very quickly.) I heard slurping sounds at my feet as my black socks became saliva sponges. I was no longer trying to untie myself. Instead, I found that I loved each leg of the journey I had been taken on. Approximately ten minutes later it happened again. I shot my load. The person underneath my legs sucking me swallowed the small amount of cum that squirted from my cock. I shook and trembled in ecstasy as his tongue continued to probe in and out of my piss hole.

When my body stopped shaking I was helped back into a normal sitting position and the gag was removed from my mouth. Before I could say anything though a cup was put to my lips and I was forced to drink a tasteless liquid. I suddenly felt very drowsy. Supposedly this was the same stuff that had been used to drug my food. I fell asleep.

When I came to it was one AM (according to my desk clock.) I was completely untied, the blindfold and gag removed, and my clothing was on me. I lifted my head up from the desk and thought that it had been a dream. Sure, that's it, a dream.

Working a double shift had knocked the crap out of me and I fell asleep at my desk. I continued reassuring myself until I saw the pile of discarded rope under my desk.

The Morning After
(Canadian Prince)

Author: Christopher Trevor

I woke up around 8:00 AM on Sunday morning. As I opened my eyes and looked around the hotel room, which was dimly lit from the sun peeking through the window shades I smiled from ear to ear, a feeling of overwhelming joy, bliss and ecstasy coursing through my very being. I stretched on my back, squirmed a bit under the sheets and turned my head to look at the handsome man sleeping next to me. I took in the sight of Dave, my handsome, handsome buddy from Canada, my Canadian prince as I had nicknamed him, because in my eyes and in my heart, that is what he is, a prince. He is a prince in every sense of the word. Looking at his handsome face as he slept, him looking at me in his sleep, a small smile playing on his face, lying on his side, my heart swelled, my heart rate accelerated and my cock stiffened, even though Dave and I had both cum twice the night before, when we had gotten back to the hotel room after dinner and the Broadway show we had seen.

I gently, so as not to wake Dave just yet, sat up on the king-sized bed and continued taking in the sight of my sleeping Canadian prince. He was breathing evenly and with a sound of contentment, his mouth now slightly open. I wondered if he was dreaming. I reached around him and gently trailed my fingertips against his white hair on the back of his neck. His hair was soft to the touch, and oh how I loved running my fingers through it when Dave would kiss me, (and My God, but I am happy to say that my Canadian prince LOVED kissing me, and I admit that the taste of his tongue in my mouth was sweet ecstasy every time he did kiss me) how I loved the feel of his soft white hair on the back of his strong neck as I squeezed and kneaded that neck.

Dave squirmed a bit in his sleep as I gently trailed my fingertips over the hair on the back of his neck, and then he pushed the blankets down a bit, exposing his upper torso, his hairy well-defined muscular chest, his spectacularly sized round pointy pink nipples, nipples that I could nurse on, slurp at and suck all day, all day suckers, that were Dave's nipples. And Dave loved having his nipples worked on in any way shape or form that I wished; it was one of his weaknesses after all. And I was only too happy to oblige the handsome guy in working his nipples for him. The way he moaned contentedly when I worked his nipples, the way his cock stiffened at the touch of my mouth on his nipples, it all added up to heightened ecstasy for both of us. I loved how hard and leathery feeling Dave's nipples became as I worked them orally more and more. In my opinion Dave's nipples are hot-wired to his cock. Dave's shoulders are broad and strong, wide as a doorway; his arms are well-defined and muscular, beautiful in their muscularity. For his maturity and age Dave was a gem, and when he had first sent me a picture of him wearing nothing but a Speedo bikini, when we had met online, well, if you believe in love or lust at first sight, that is exactly what happened. To tell it plainly Dave has a smile like sunshine and the way he was smiling in the picture he had sent me told me that he was an all-around nice person, a gentle person and a loving person…and perhaps an adventurous person as well?

As I sat with my back against the bed-board Dave slowly woke up, and like me he stretched a bit and squirmed around on the bed. I watched delightedly as the muscles in my Canadian prince's arms flexed a bit, what a sight. As he squirmed around on the bed and seemed to writhe a bit I stole a glance at our discarded tuxedos, Dave's bowtie, my underpants, Dave's red Speedo that he had been wearing under his tuxedo the previous night and our shoes and MY black silk tall dress socks.

All of it was strewn on the floor near the bed, seeing as Dave and I had hastily undressed each other the night before, being that we were so ravenous for each other.

I grinned a bit at Dave's red Speedo on the floor, thinking how sexy and unconventional it was the night before for him to have been wearing it under his tuxedo, rather than a pair of traditional men's briefs or boxer shorts. But Speedos are Dave's fetish and he loves wearing them for all occasions, especially sexual occasions, and when we first met I was only too happy and thrilled to introduce the Canadian prince to a few of my fetishes as well.

Dave turned onto his back, opened his eyes, looked up at me, and smiled with his lips pressed together.

"Good morning," I said, smiling joyfully and I trailed a fingertip against Dave's cheek, my heart melting at his handsomeness, that innocence that he projects. "Did you sleep well my Canadian prince?"

"Good morning to you as well my USA stud, and yes, I slept very well," Dave replied, took my finger that was against his face in my hand, gently kissed the tip of it a few times and then sucked on it a bit as well, sending chills through me. "The play we saw was great, thanks so much again for getting us the tickets to that and dinner before the show in that old fashioned steak house was wonderful as well. It was truly a really romantic evening out in New York City with you my USA stud."

"And dressed to the nines at that," I said, reached over to the night table on my side of the bed and held up my undone long silk bowtie from the evening before.

"Yes, wearing black Armani tuxedos really lent the evening a feeling of flair and regality," Dave said, turned onto his stomach, crawled atop my lower body and gripped my sides in his strong hands, his face and mouth making a beeline for my nipples it seemed. "Did you see how the girls across from ours in that steak house were taking in the sight of us?"

I smiled even more and gently stroked the back of Dave's neck, loving the feel of the soft hair back there and said, "My feeling is that they were taking in the sight of YOU my Canadian prince. You see, I don't think you realize just how very handsome, debonair and irresistible you really are. Young women adore men your age, especially men your age who are so very beguilingly handsome."

With that, Dave gripped my sides tighter, strongly in his firm grasp and pressed his lips against one of my already jutted up nipples. I gasped as he slurped my left sided nipple into his mouth, teased it with his tongue and gently nipped at it with his front-most teeth.

Dave's grip on me was like iron and usually it was me who worked on his nipples, but my Canadian prince suddenly working on my nipple the way he was didn't hurt all that much in the department of my piss hard erection. The sounds of slurping filled the room and Dave's head bobbed up and down and back and forth as he feasted like a madman on my nipple. When he switched to the other one I gripped the back of his neck with both hands then, writhed under him and roared in a man's passion, for my right-sided nipple is oh so much more sensitive feeling than the left one.

"Oh holy fuck, what a good morning this really is my Canadian prince," I huffed breathlessly and wriggled like a fish out of water underneath Dave as he devoured my nipples, making sounds of hunger and manly famine as he sent my cock to a state beyond piss hardness.

My cock was throbbing and pulsing with a life of its own and I could feel it oozing pre cum like mad under the covers.

"Oh God Dave, my Dave," I whispered as tears of joy and sheer ecstasy flowed from the sides of my eyes as I lay with the back of my head pressed hard against my pillow and Dave worked his magic on me mouth-wise.

After my nipples had suffered in the throes of unbelievable ecstasy for a good fifteen minutes or so Dave abandoned them and began kissing and nipping, gently biting me down my chest area to my stomach region, the palms of his strong hands now pressed against the sheets and blankets as he pulled himself up to his knees over me. As he got himself better situated on the bed my Canadian prince kicked the sheets and blankets out from behind him and then there they were, his exquisitely shaped, beautiful tuxedo OTC sheer socked feet. Knowing my strong fetish for sheer thick and thin tuxedo socks Dave had left his sheers on the night before during our evening romp in the bed and after we had fallen asleep. At the sight of his socked feet, his strong calves encased in the see-thru silk my heart accelerated even more, if that were possible, and I reached over to my night table and grabbed my long discarded silk black bowtie. Before I shot my load I had to regain control of this situation, and I DID NOT want to cum just yet that morning. You see, even before Dave had begun his devouring of my nipples and teasing of my chest and stomach areas I had other plans in mind for when we had woken up that Sunday morning in our hotel room in New York City.

As Dave was heading for my cock and balls, ready obviously to devour and tease them and make me shoot an early morning load I reached forward and looped two strands of my long silk black bowtie around his left wrist and pulled it tight.

Dave looked at his suddenly silk looped wrist and then up at me as I was breathing heavily, a look of total determination etched on my face. He grinned and said, "Well my USA stud, it would seem you have some plans for me this morning. A continuation of last evening I'm guessing?"

"You know it my Canadian prince," I replied with a grin of my own, a rather evil looking grin, actually and yanked Dave toward me using the slack about his wrist as a leash of sorts.

"Oh my," Dave muttered and grinned.

Seconds later Dave was on his knees on the bed, his socked feet and calves tucked under him, facing me and looking a tad frightened and excited at the same time, behind the red silk blindfold I had tied over his eyes…as he held his wrists together in front of him and I looped and looped and tied and tied my long silk bowtie around and around those wrists of my Canadian prince's…

"Should have known you would want me all bound up my USA stud," Dave said, sounding nervous and inquisitive at the same time. "I wonder what you have in mind for me now… I'm sure like always it will be exhilarating yet somehow fear-provoking for me at the same time."

"Oh yes Dave, you've got that right, so very right," I responded and gently kissed his blindfolded eyes, breathing in my Canadian prince's early morning and rested scent.

Once Dave's wrists were tied good and tight, but not so tight as to cut off his blood circulation, I hooked a hand around the back of his neck, moved his head forward and rested his forehead on one of my shoulders, as I gently and lovingly caressed the soft white hair on the back of his neck. Oh my God, and how I loved the sight of the knot of a blindfold tied behind Dave's head and pressing against that soft white delectable hair of his, sweetness defined.

On the times when I have decided to blindfold Dave for my kinky sort of games that he has allowed me to play with him since we met, he has found how not being able to see what I am going to do to him next intensifies the experience only about a thousand percent.

And not to mention the fact that Dave looks awesomely erotic, submissive, helpless and mysterious with a blindfold tied over his eyes. Back when Dave and I first met online and when I saw the way he was smiling in the picture of himself wearing nothing but a Speedo that he had sent me, well, for whatever the reason, I instantly pictured the handsome Canadian guy tied up and blindfolded while I sucked and slurped and nursed on his big round pointy nipples, and that was just to get the party going.

As I gently stroked the soft white hair on the back of Dave's neck and toyed with the knot in his red silk blindfold my Canadian prince moved his tied up hands to my chest and squeezed one of my nipples with his thumbs and first fingers.

"You're really after those nips of mine this morning aren't you my Canadian prince?" I asked Dave teasingly, leaned back and grabbed his bound wrists tightly in both my hands, moving his bound up wrists upwards and toward the bed-board, stretching Dave out on his back as I went.

All of the fantasies that I imagined with Dave, the man who loved to be sexed over in his Speedos, ran in the direction of the erotic. I wanted to see him tied up, blindfolded, gagged, helpless, and totally at my mercy. I felt that having Dave in that position would show me just how gentle and loving he really was, because I felt that the look of fear on his face would melt my heart, sounds strange I realize, but it makes sense to me. And allowing me to do these things to Dave would prove to him that I could be trusted totally, but with just that little smidgen of doubt thrown in, to add some sexual tension to each experience we would share.

A few short minutes later I had Dave's wrists tied to the bed-board, him all stretched out on the bed on his ripped and muscular back, looking devilishly sexy and helpless at the same time.

"Got me in your clutches again my USA stud," Dave muttered as I delighted in straightening out his sheer OTC socks and pulling them up for him as well.

"You will *always* be in my clutches Dave," I replied happily, squeezing my Canadian prince's socked ankles. "Now, what say we have some early morning fun before a hearty breakfast in the hotel's dining room, yes?"

"Oh yes, yes, definitely," Dave panted, not really being in a position to argue at the moment. "Please yes…"

So, after a month or so of getting to know each other online, after many, many IM sessions where we role-played our erotic fantasies, Dave detailing his fantasies of being sexed over and sexing someone over while in just a Speedo, or briefs, or even long sexy underwear… him telling me how he loved the feel of the silky material against his skin; and then, me throwing in my erotic fantasies of bondage, but promising to never, ever hurt the guy, Dave and I struck up a wonderful friendship…and now, for the first time, here we were together, in the flesh (literally) in a hotel room, and in the heart of Times Square in New York city.

After I had straightened out and pulled up Dave's sheer OTC black tuxedo socks I gripped his calves tight, pushed his legs up as high as possible to expose his bunghole and dove in headfirst.

"OHHHHHH, OH MY GOD," Dave bantered, sounding like he was in a total sexual tizzy as I held his legs up, the bottoms of his feet looking up at the ceiling, as I buried my nose and mouth in his gaping asshole, tonguing him, slurping at his ass walls and sucking his hole for all I was worth. "Oh my USA stud you are driving me insane this morning…just as you did last night…just as you always do…all the time you drive me insane…with ecstasy…"

I ran the palms of my hands up and down Dave's silk socked calves, they felt like iron under my touch, and the sounds of my slurping hungrily at my Canadian prince's asshole intensified, as did Dave's rants and roars of a man's passion.

"OHHH you-YOU'RE making me into a nut here Christopher," Dave swooned as I flicked my tongue rapidly over his ass walls, teasing him mercilessly as I did so.

Holding his legs up higher a few moments later I slathered my tongue up and down Dave's ass cheeks, drooling on them as I did so and lapping up my saliva like a canine in heat.

Dave arched his blindfolded head back a bit against the bed-board and made guttural sounds from deep in his throat as I kissed and pecked his ass cheeks, resumed eating his asshole and sucking at it and flicked my tongue over and over his velvety ass walls. Just to make Dave even crazier and to make his head spin even more, I spit liberally a few times into his hole, which had become like a spittoon of sorts at that moment. And when I pressed my lips tightly against Dave's spittoon/ hole and sucked my saliva back out again, well, the guy made mewling sounds that I had never heard before. Needless to say my Canadian prince had broken out in goose bumps. He writhed on the bed, squirmed in a mixture of passion and anxiety as he struggled against the binding ropes and panted about how he wanted to, needed to, and just had to, shoot his load. It was just what I wanted to hear… because it was just what I was not going to permit my Canadian prince to do…at least not yet.

After I had licked, sucked, slurped and flicked my tongue around in Dave's asshole for about fifteen solid minutes, I ordered my Canadian prince to hold his legs up on his own for a few seconds and to spread them as wide as he possibly could, telling him that I had yet another surprise in store for him where his sweet hole was concerned. Panting as if he had been jogging for hours in the heat Dave murmured about not having any choice but to do as I was telling him to do…and I cannot describe for you just how very sexy and stimulating he then looked as he poked his long legs into the air and spread them wide and wider, revealing more and more of that beautiful asshole of his. Dave's socked feet stared upwards and he curled his toes back a bit as he formed a wide letter "Y" with his spread legs.

"Good boy Dave," I said. "Now here comes my next surprise."

That said, I inserted a battery powered pink colored good sized butt-plug into my Canadian prince's love tunnel.

"AWWWWW GODDD, oh my God, oh my hole," Dave squabbled in total heated passion as I slid the device home in him, the shaft of it kissing his ass walls, massaging them as it went in inch by pleasurable inch and when the flat base of it snapped home my Canadian prince clenched his teeth tight. "RRRRRHHHHH…looks like you got more kinky stuff in mind for me this morning my hot, hot, fucking USA stud…"

"You don't need three guesses to know that my Canadian prince," I taunted Dave and gave the butt-plug wedged in him a few good twists and turns, getting some more loud guttural throaty sounds out of my captive.

I slowly lowered Dave's legs back down to the bed, massaged them a bit to make sure he didn't cramp at all…

…he thanked me, and then looked somehow dismayed yet even more aroused when he felt me wrapping and looping white cotton rope around his sheer silk black socked feet.

"AW God, tying me up some more my USA stud," Dave breathed heavily, his lips quivering as he spoke.

As I tied his socked feet Dave's erection was like a pre cum dripping skyscraper between his sexy tree-trunk like well-muscled legs.

"How does that butt-plug feel in your hole my Canadian prince?" I asked Dave as I finished tying his socked feet, and then playfully squeezed his toes a few times and kissed the tops of his feet as well, inhaling the musty scent emanating from them.

"F-feels amazing, I feel so filled up back there, oh my, Christopher, the things you do to me, like nothing I've ever known before," Dave panted, the sounds of anguish in his voice and I saw tears were staining his red silk blindfold.

"Glad you like it Dave, because now here comes part two of my butt-plug surprise for you," I said and if Dave hadn't been blindfolded he would have seen the wicked look in my eyes as I picked up the remote control device for the battery powered butt-plug.

I clicked it onto a medium setting, just to get Dave's asshole and ass walls really simmering.

The vibrating sound of buzzing suddenly filled the room and Dave instantly clenched his bound hands into big fists, clenched his teeth again and roared, "RRRRRRRHHHHH, ARRRRHHH fuccccckkk, CHRISTOPHER, oh my USA stud, that's a damned vibrating butt-plug you shoved in me bud...AAAAARRRHHHH YESSSSSSS YESSSSSS..."

Smiling even more evilly I lay down next to my Canadian prince on my side and slurped one of his man-sized tits into my mouth, slurping it against my front-most teeth, sucked it and trailed my fingertips gently and teasingly along the bottom-side of Dave's erect cock shaft.

"OOOOOO...teasing me so lovingly, want to cum, you're going to make me cum," Dave bantered breathlessly and I lessened my intensity of my fingers trailing along my Canadian prince's cock shaft. "OHHHHH no, no, don't stop, please Christopher, PLEASE, that thing in my hole feels like thousands of bees buzzing in me, and it's making me crazy, I JUST HAVE TO CUM...please, work my cock as well as my tits, oh please my USA stud, please..."

As I suckled Dave's tit and softly, oh so softly teased his cock with my fingertips he oozed dollops of pre cum, he seethed with clenched teeth and tried unsuccessfully to get his hands free of the bindings.

"OH God, what you're doing to me along with what that vibrating device in me is doing to me, you're sending me over the edge Christopher," Dave cried.

I stopped suckling his tit and whispered, "You can probably cum without your cock even being touched Dave, my beautiful Canadian prince…"

With that I took my fingers away from Dave's cock, he screamed out, "NO, NO, please Christopher," and I suddenly gave his tit that I had been sucking a hard squeeze and twist.

"ARRRRRHHHH GODDDDD…" was Dave's response and that was all it took.

Without me even touching his steely erect cock, Dave squirmed and screamed on the bed as his cock let loose with torrents of his Canadian slop, all over his chest and stomach areas. As he shot his load and shot his load I clicked the remote control to a higher setting and the buzzing in Dave's asshole intensified.

"Oh you devil, you trickster," Dave ranted and stomped his tied socked feet up and down on the bed, yanking crazily at the ropes binding his wrists, and he came even harder as the buzzing against his ass walls drove him into frenzy-mode.

When I saw that his spurts were dying down I quickly untied Dave's feet, ready to take the buzzing butt-plug from his hole, because, like any other guy out there, after Dave shoots his load his asshole (and other tender parts of him as well) become super-sensitive to the touch, and having a buzzing butt-plug in his hole would not feel all that good at that point, hardy fucking HAR, HAR…

So, as Dave shot what I thought would be the last of his load I slowly extracted the butt-plug from his love tunnel. To my utter shock, once the butt-plug was out Dave let out another guttural sounding roar and a rope of cum squirted from his cock that was longer and thicker than all the ones he had squirted previously.

"Oh my God," I whispered and when Dave was done creaming he lay there sweating, gasping for breath, crying behind his blindfold and shaking like a leaf.

"PL-please Christopher, please, oh please untie me buddy," Dave pleaded and I instantly undid the silk bowtie that held his wrists tied to the bed-board.

Dave lowered his blindfold, let his eyes adjust back to the light and looked at me hungrily.

"You okay my Canadian prince?" I asked Dave, grinning at him comically.

"Fucker, tortured the fuck out of me.. again, just like last night, just like every time since we first met," Dave ranted at me. "Tie me up, blindfold me, gag me, and make me wear my Speedos and dress socks, torment me...GOD...Now you shove a damned buzzer up my hole to force me to cum like a banshee...Holy God.. "

I thought for sure that Dave was pissed with me, that he was about to tell me to take a hike and that we would never see each other again. I was thinking that maybe I had gone too far this time in my teasing and tormenting my Canadian prince.

But then, Dave leaned forward, grabbed me under my arms and pulled me toward him. Before I could react my Canadian prince had his mouth pressed hard against mine and his tongue was snaking its way in. He kissed me long and hard, sucked my tongue and trailed his tongue tip along my gums and all over the inside of my mouth. I made groaning sounds as he hugged me so tight that I thought he would literally smother me to death.

When Dave stopped kissing me he held me tight against himself, hugged me and said in a brusque tone of voice, "Why do you always think I'm pissed off at you my USA stud? I let you tie me up for Christ's sake. So there's no way I can be pissed off by the things you decide to visit on me."

We smiled at each other devilishly and laughed a bit...and then I picked up the rope from the bed that I has used to tie Dave's feet with.

"Aw no, me and big mouth," Dave said sarcastically.

Moments later I had Dave's wrists tied back to the bed-board, as I straddled him, standing over my Canadian prince on the bed, thrusting my hard cock in and out of his most willing, yet somehow unwilling mouth, feeding him my man stick over and over again.

"Oh yeah, my fucking beautiful Canadian prince's mouth, my handsome mature Speedo man, eat my cock, suck my cock, lick my cock, I demanded meanly.

I slathered my pre cum oozing cock tip over and over Dave's lips. He kissed and flicked his tongue over it, ate my pre cum and then I plunged my throbbing erection back into his craw. Dave's jaws ballooned at the sides of his face as he sucked me like a madman, my low hanging balls crashing against his chin, goose bumps now breaking out all over me as I headed toward a man-sized gusher.

"Why in all fucks do you tie me up for this?" Dave asked as my cock dangled in front of his mouth for a moment while I let him catch his breath. "You know how much I love working your… RRRMMMFFFF…"

But before Dave could finish his sentence I had again filled his mouth with my cock.

"RRRHHHMMFFF…" Dave squawked as I then began shooting my load. "UUUHHMMMFFFFF…"

"Oh fuck yeah, that's it my Canadian prince, eat my USA load of slop, chow down on that breakfast appetizer," I grunted, spearing Dave's mouth meanly with my cock at that point, slamming into his mouth almost.

Dave did just as I directed and literally gulped down the torrents of my mess, some of it oozing out the sides of his mouth, which made for a pretty sexy picture let me tell you.

When I was done Dave did not ask to be untied this time, it seems it's always after HE cums that he wants to be free of bondage. But after I had made the guy guzzle down my mess of ball juice he simply sat there tied to the bed-board with his head hanging down, his tongue hanging out of his mouth with remnants of my cum all over it and catching his breath.

"Oh my Canadian prince, don't get too comfortable just yet, we're still not done yet," I said, sounding menacing.

Dave looked up at me and asked, "WH-what do you mean? I really need to piss at this point and..."

"So do I," I exclaimed and inserted just the very tip of my flaccid cock into Dave's mouth, resting it gently on his tongue.

With my cock in his mouth again, but not hard this time, Dave looked up at me quizzically; and then a look of disbelief filled his beautiful eyes as I began trickling my piss into his mouth.

"Hrrrmmmfff????" Dave asked but then pulled his jaws in like he was sipping from a straw and drank down my rank offering, sending chills through me as he sipped.

I watched as Dave closed his eyes, a look of ecstasy filling his face as he drank down the yellow stream emanating from my cock.

"Good boy," I whispered. "Oh my Canadian prince, how I adore you..."

A short while later I walked beside Dave as we both headed to the luxurious bathroom of our hotel suite, to shower together and without a doubt to enjoy more kinky moments together that morning, and all before breakfast at that...

Draining Dave

Author: Christopher Trevor

"OOOOOO, oh my Lord, oh my USA stud, OOOOOOO…" Dave moaned and groaned in his sexy sounding guttural throaty voice as I slowly and methodically sucked his big cock and licked his balls alternately.

And when I said that I was working my Canadian prince slowly, I meant it, slowly being the key word here, because that was EXACTLY what I was doing, slowly leading my handsome Dave toward orgasm, and it would be a gusher that would make his teeth itch.

"OOOOOOOO Christopher, the way you work me over, the things you do to me, it's all like some kind of sinister magic that you've visited upon me.

"I'll take as a compliment my Canadian prince," I said with a grin on my face, gripped Dave's HUGELY erect cock by the shaft and gave it a few tugs, jiggles and twists and then let go of it, only to let it twitch in the wind as I knelt under my Canadian prince and again lapped hungrily at his balls, drooling on them, drenching them with my saliva.

Dave was positioned standing in front of me in the center of our luxurious hotel suite. His hands were locked behind him in a pair of old-fashioned steel handcuffs, the key for which was nearby on an end table, and you can take this to the bank for sure, Dave was looking longingly over at that key, the key to his freedom. As I licked the Canadian prince's balls and then sucked them alternately Dave's head spun and he wiggled oh so sexily in front of me. My handsome and mature Canadian prince was scantily clad in nothing more than a pair of OTC navy blue nylon dress socks and a tight red Speedo bikini that was pulled down in front and tucked under his aching testicles.

"OH man, when I was done showering and when I came out of the bathroom in my Speedo and I saw you toying with those handcuffs and dress socks I knew I was in for some more of your trickery my USA stud." Dave said to me breathlessly.

In response I said, "You love my trickery Dave," and leaned upward and greedily slurped Dave's pre cum dripping erection once more into my mouth.

"YUHHHHHHHH..." Dave groaned and arched his back a bit, his nipples jutting up on his chest and pointing upward as I sucked him like a bit of a madman.

Before breakfast that morning I wanted an appetizer...and Dave's cock and balls were the only thing on the menu at the moment.

Dave swooned on his socked feet, gyrating his well-toned muscular body and swiveled his cock around and around in my mouth as I dribbled on it, swirled my tongue around it with his rhythmic moves and ran my hands up and down his navy blue socked calves, loving the feel of the thin nylon over his iron-like calves. I teased Dave a bit by then sucking only on the very tip of his cock, sending shockwaves of chills through his beautifully shaped body.

"ARRRRRRRHHH, no fair, no fair my USA stud, I can't possibly cum if you only suck the tip of my cock," Dave seethed down at me.

"And you won't cum till I say so my Canadian prince," I responded, looking up at Dave with that glint in my eyes that makes Dave wonder why in all hell he allowed me to restrain him yet again, wondering, always wondering.

To put it plainly I adore the guy more than he will ever know, and during the times that I have him restrained, whether it's in ropes, leather restraints, or handcuffs like I presently had him in, he knows that I would never bring ANY harm to him whatsoever.

It's just that, as I have explained before, when Dave and I had first met online and he had sent me pictures of him wearing nothing more than sexy Speedos, for whatever the reason I instantly pictured him in those Speedos…and tied up and at my mercy. And to also put it plainly, Dave loves being at my mercy. If he didn't I doubt he would submit to my ropes and games.

As Dave danced a sexy dance on his socked toes while I sucked just the tip of his cock I slowly slid my mouth back over his shaft, engulfing his erection again in the warmth of the hole in my face.

"HUHHHHHH, HUHHHHH, OH MY GOD," Dave gasped and shuddered, goose bumps breaking out all over him.

As I sucked his cock, thrusting him in and out of my mouth I gently massaged Dave's saliva soaked balls with my fingertips.

"You're driving me crazy Christopher," Dave moaned, his lips quivering madly.

After I sucked Dave once more to the point that he was near to shooting his load I frustrated the guy again by sliding his skyscraper of an erection out of my mouth and watched from my kneeling position as it twitched and danced between his oh so sexy legs. When a few droplets of pre cum appeared at his dick slit I slurped them off and gulped them down, savoring the taste of Canadian prince pre seed.

I gripped Dave's socked calves again and pressed my nose and mouth against the warmth of his low hanging testicles, also taking in the scent of his manliness that was all over the red Speedo that was tucked under his balls. I slithered my tongue over my Canadian prince's balls slowly, methodically teasing them. As I did so it was oh so entertaining to watch his erection twitch and ooze more pre cum in a state of frustration.

"OOOOOOOOO…I am so close, but so far," Dave whispered. "Want to cum so bad…"

"Not yet my Canadian prince, oh not yet, I'm having too much fun tormenting you," I replied and trailed my fingers against the underside of Dave's Speedo, right under his ass crack.

"OOOOOOOOO, OH CHRISTOPHER," Dave railed and hoisted himself right up on his tiptoes.

I giggled a bit and as I teased Dave's ass crack through his Speedo and as he danced a dance of helplessness up on his socked tiptoes I again slurped just the tip of his cock between my lips…and this time I did something really mean to the poor guy… I jiggled my tongue tip against his piss hole, which made him shiver as if he were outside naked in a snowstorm.

"OHHHHHH you sexy devil, my USA stud," Dave whimpered and tears filled his eyes.

He hunched his broad shoulders up and clenched his handcuffed hands into a big fist. As I poked my tongue tip against Dave's piss hole I once more tasted his pre cum and even some droplets of piss. As my Canadian prince gasped for breath his muscular chest jutted forward, those tits of his teasing me as I teased his cock and balls and ass crack.

"FUCKER…" Dave whimpered when I let his cock tip slide out from between my lips, I grabbed his throbbing erection again in my fist and jiggled it, twisted it and stroked it, three times each only. "OH you have me balanced on the edge of a sexual cliff my USA stud, and I'm about to plunge right off it…oh please Christopher, how much longer till you allow me to cum???"

"I think the real question here is how much longer can I tease and frustrate and torment you my Canadian prince?" I replied.

Dave grinned down at me and said, "As you would say in your books Christopher, this is a shitty way to treat a prince of any kind, even a Canadian one."

"A VERY hot and beautiful Canadian one," I replied and gobbled Dave's erection fully into my mouth...AGAIN...

"YUHHHHHHHH...and here I go again, helplessly to the land of Ecstasy with my USA stud," Dave thundered. "NEED to cum... NEED to shoot my load of Canadian slop..."

As I ravenously sucked Dave's cock and trailed the palms of my hands up and down his sexy socked calves I made my plans for how to torment the guy next...and to make him wait even more to cum...

A few scant moments later I had Dave blindfolded with a white silk neckerchief/scarf that he had worn the night before along with his tuxedo and facing away from me and staring at a blank wall in our suite. Kneeling behind Dave I slowly and bit by bit peeled his red Speedo away from his ass cheeks and moved it lovingly down his long sexy legs. As I moved the Speedo down over his socked calves my heart-rate accelerated. Dave obligingly lifted one foot at a time to step out of the Speedo, leaving him clad now in just his tall navy blue dress socks. At the sight of my Canadian prince's creamy white coconut shaped ass cheeks I could not resist the urge to tease the handsome guy some more, and STILL not let him cum.

"AAAAHHHHHHHH, OOOOOOOOO, how you love doing that to me my USA stud," Dave thundered seconds later as I was now gripping his ass cheeks, splayed them apart to expose his pink bunghole and was flicking and jetting my tongue around in there like crazy. "And how I love to have you work my hole over this way, it simply drives me into a heated frenzy. And not being able to see you at it does indeed make it all the more intense...as you know."

I chuckled a bit and buried my nose and mouth in Dave's rectal opening...

I gripped handfuls of Dave's soft skinned tight ass cheeks till they were red in my grasps and flicked my tongue hard against his ass walls, breathing in his manly and at the same time raunchy scent back there. Dave's cock was so hard at that point that the tip of it was pressing against the wall I had my Canadian prince standing in front of.

"OOOOOOOOO…what you're doing to me…I swear, I could cum without my cock even being touched my USA stud," Dave blubbered, crying tears of joy behind his white silk blindfold.

"Well then, in that case," I said and holding Dave's ass cheeks super-tight in my grasps I moved him a few tiny steps away from the wall, so that his erection was now simply wallowing in the wind once more.

"OH me and my big mouth," Dave said with a wide smile on his blindfolded face as I quickly gave his asshole a few loud slurpy and syrupy kisses, really sending chills through the poor frustrated and beyond horned guy at that point.

Large dollops of my saliva dripped from Dave's hole as I meanly hummed into it, making vibrating sorts of sounds back there, causing Dave to make sounds like "AYYYYYY" and "EEEEEEERRRR" as I played his asshole like it was some sort of kinky musical instrument.

"Y-you're making me crazy here, totally crazy," Dave said in a high-pitched tone of voice. "PLEASE Christopher, oh please my USA stud, please release me from this torment…oh please…"

The sounds of Dave pleading broke my heart…and boned me up like you can't believe…

"ARRRRRHHHH oh yes, yes, please don't stop this time my USA stud," Dave was crooning and pleading a short while later, after I had propped his back against the wall he had been facing and whipped his blindfold off him.

Dancing on his socked tiptoes as I stood at his side holding him by one nipple with my thumb and first fingers of one hand and stroking his pounding erection with my other hand, my Canadian prince's own pre cum acting as a lube of sorts, he railed and thundered madly.

"OHHHHHHHH, OOOOOOO OH MY LORD, I don't think I've ever been so worked up before my USA stud," Dave exclaimed crazily, looking downward, his chin resting at the top of his chest, watching as I stroked his cock and teased his nipple with my fingers and thumb. "This blast off is going to be one for the history books..."

The sounds of squishing filled the air as I stroked Dave's pre cum lubed cock and the smell of pre cum was redolent as well as I went on my stroking my Canadian prince harder and harder. He looked upwards, gasped loudly for breath, pressed the back of his head against the wall and tears of joy filled his eyes.

"My USA stud, oh Christopher, Christopher," Dave whined joyfully.

I stroked him harder yet and then my Canadian prince cried out, "I'm cumming, oh God, I am going to cum so hard my USA stud, my Christopher..."

I let go of Dave's nipple and his cock, dropped to my knees in front of him and slurped his cock into my mouth. No way was I going to waste his good stuff...

Dave was correct, his gusher was indeed one for the history books, and he shot his load and shot his load and shot his load, faster than I could gulp it down as he did...

"ARRRRRRRRRHHHH GODDDDDD, Never shot such a hefty load, and so soon after cumming earlier, RRRRRRHHHHHH my USA stud, the things you to do me, UN-FUCKING-BELIEVABLE..." Dave roared like a captured marine as I sucked him and siphoned more of his good stuff from him.

"You've made edging and teasing me into a new sort of art form," Dave exclaimed seconds later as his orgasm started to slow down...and I was able to scoff down the last of his spurts.

As his orgasm tapered off and his cock softened and shriveled in my mouth Dave was, as usual, gasping and heaving for breath. As I gently caressed his socked calves and squeezed them a bit I gave my Canadian prince's spent testicles a few good licks and kisses.

"Christopher, oh my Lord, oh my USA stud," Dave whimpered.

But before the guy could demand to be freed from the bondage I had him in I quickly slurped just the very tip of his soft slimy cum coated cock into my mouth, wrapping my lips tightly around it.

"YUHHHHHH...oh what now, what the fuck now???" Dave panted and slammed his muscular back against the wall.

More goose bumps broke out all over my Canadian prince's muscular body with what I did to him next, namely, began poking my tongue tip into his piss slit, teasing his need to piss.

Dave so sexily arched his head back, pursed his lips together and breathed heavily through his nose, knowing where I was leading him now.

"OH MY GAWWWDDD..." Dave seethed scant seconds later and began a slow trickle piss.

I kept my lips wrapped firmly around his cock tip and sucked slowly, as if I were drinking through a straw, driving my Canadian prince back to intense heights of passion.

"OH LORD, never felt so good to piss," Dave murmured, sweating in his socks at that point, as I scoffed down his Canadian yellow stream. "That felt almost as good as shooting my load Christopher."

When I was done I got to my feet, sauntered over to where the key to the handcuffs was and picked it up. As I walked back over to Dave and saw the way he was gasping for air, heaving in a sexual frenzy I wished that I could keep him handcuffed for the rest of the day and simply tease and work him over some more and more. But we were in New York on a vacation after all...and Dave had traveled all the way from Canada to be with me...and while he enjoyed my kinky games of bondage he wasn't in New York to be tied up the entire time, although the idea of that was mesmerizing, LOL.

After I freed Dave from the handcuffs, I watched as he sat down to remove the navy blue socks he had on…dropped them on the floor, and still catching his breath he walked naked to the luxury bathroom in our suite to take another shower before breakfast.

Smiling from ear to ear with tears of joy in my eyes I picked up Dave's blue socks, pressed them to my nose and mouth, inhaled his manly feet scent and my cock grew stiff again…

The Story of Vinny

Author: Christopher Trevor

"I'm really glad you two guys are here, because I want to tell you a story," I said slowly to my two best buddies as we sat in the living room of my condominium apartment. "You see, I've kept this story to myself for more than two years now and I think it's time that I finally told it to someone. You two being my two best friends, well I want to, no, more like I need to tell you about it."

"It doesn't sound like it's going to be a happy story," Don said to me, looking across the room at me.

Don is extremely handsome, five feet ten inches tall, with wavy blond hair and piercing blue eyes. He works as a bank auditor and I've seen the looks the ladies give him when we are out after work having drinks and he's still dressed in his suit and tie.

"It's not a happy story," I replied. "As a matter of fact, it's a horror story of sorts, the only difference is, is that this is a real life horror story."

"I love horror stories," Robert said enthusiastically.

Robert is handsome like Don, but in a more rugged looking way. He has dark brown hair cut short, chestnut shaped brown eyes and stands five feet nine inches tall. His job as a construction worker keeps him in great shape, which, unlike Don, who works out in a gym on a regular basis.

"I'm glad you like horror stories Robert, but unfortunately for someone this horror story is, as I said, *true,*" I said to Robert and took a sip of my club soda. "I suppose I want to tell it because relating it to people that I trust will be a form of therapy for me."

"Tell it Chris," Don said, looking at me quizzically.

"Do you remember my friend Vinny?" I asked them.

"Sure," Don replied. "He was your neighbor from upstairs on the third floor. He moved to California."

"He didn't actually move, more like he ran," I said.

"Ran?" Robert asked in disbelief. "Why?"

"Well, Vinny had told everyone that he had been offered a good job in California and that was why he went," I said. "The truth was he ran to California to escape the demons that plagued him here."

"What the fuck are you talking about?" Robert asked. "What demons?"

"Memories, horrible memories of a horrible, horrible day," I responded slowly for emphasis. "You see, Vinny had been abducted by two men while on his way to work one morning, two VERY nasty and horrible men. They kept Vinny prisoner for an entire day, abused him sexually, worked him over big time, tortured the fuck out of him and out-rightly raped him, over and over again."

"*Shit,*" Don said, with a look of disbelief on his handsome face. "And he told you about it?"

I nodded.

"Didn't he report it to the police?" Robert asked.

"No," I replied. "Vinny felt that they wouldn't believe him. He said that the cops would more than likely say that things like that don't happen to men, especially men as big, muscular and mean as Vinny."

I leaned back on the couch and looked sadly at my two friends.

"So, do you want to hear it?" I asked them, but not looking happy or all that anxious to tell the story.

They both nodded. I took a breath and began.

"It was a Monday morning in September, a Monday morning like any other," I began. "Vinny had to be at work early that day. He was working on a special project for the vice president of the bank he was working for. His alarm clock woke him at four AM and Vinny crawled out of bed, totally naked and walked sleepily to the bathroom for his morning shower."

"Man, I bet that would have been a sight to see," Don said with a grin on his face. "Vinny walking naked to the bathroom? YUM, I mean that guy has a hell of a fucking body, sheer rock hard muscle."

"That's very true," I said. "Anyway, Vinny showered, shaved and did whatever else he had to do in the bathroom, if you know what I mean."

My two friends nodded.

"When he was done in the bathroom Vinny went back to his bedroom to get dressed for the workday," I went on. "He told me that he chose a gray suit for that day along with a white shirt, a black silk necktie, black suede wingtip lace-up shoes and gray and black checkered cotton dress socks."

"Sounds totally fashionable," Don said to me. "He told you what he was wearing even down to his socks?"

"You'll understand why in a few moments," I said to Don.

"Vinny always liked to dress nice and fashionably," I said. "I mean, do you remember how his hair was always so slicked back and his goatee was always perfectly trimmed?"

"Sure do," Robert said. "He always looked like he'd spent hours getting dressed."

"Yeah," I said. "Well, after getting dressed Vinny put all his important papers in his attaché case and left his apartment at five AM so he could be at work very early. At five AM it was still a little dark outside and at that time this neighborhood is pretty much deserted. I mean, it's a good neighborhood, so Vinny had qualms about walking to the subway so early in the day. Besides, being built the way he is, Vinny was not worried about anyone giving him a hard time. It was the farthest thing from his mind. He didn't know though that at that moment how all that was about to change. He had walked two blocks when a big van pulled up directly next to him. The guy in the passenger seat of the van called out to Vinny, "Hey handsome guy!!" as he was leaning partly out the window. "Can you tell us how to get to twenty Third Avenue from here? Vinny, not suspecting anything untoward thought for a moment and then raised his arm, and without thinking about it stepped closer to the van, he didn't think for a second that he was in danger after all, pointing in the direction that the two men should drive in. Vinny began to say, "Go straight down this street and..." but just then the guy in the passenger seat reached out and grabbed Vinny's wrist in a tight grip. Vinny yelled things like "HEY!! And "What the fuck are you doing????" as the man quickly yanked him roughly closer to the van. The guy in the passenger seat ranted at the guy in the driver's seat, "I got him Cleeve!! I fucking got him!!" as Vinny seethed, "Let go of me you bastard!!" The guy holding Vinny's wrist yanked him further and Vinny was slammed bodily against the side of the van, HARD. Vinny gasped, totally stunned now. He dropped his attaché case to the ground, as the man in the driver's seat climbed out of the van. As the driver stepped out of the van Vinny was able to him hear him call out, "Hold him tight Otis!" with total authority in his voice."

"So, the driver of the van was named Cleeve and the guy in the passenger seat was Otis," Robert commented.

"Yeah, that's right," I said to him. "Otis held Vinny tighter than tight as Cleeve walked up to him. Cleeve looked at Vinny and said, "Handsome fucking dude you are as he ran a fingertip over Vinny's goatee. Vinny reeled and roared "Fucking bastards!!" erupting back to life in a flash. Vinny then made a fist with his free hand and as he went to punch Cleeve Otis again pulled him bodily against the van, stunning the poor guy again. Vinny cried out in pain and whispered, *"Fuckers…"* Next, Cleeve grabbed Vinny and held his huge arms tightly behind him as Otis then stepped down and out of the van. Vinny saw that the two men were both tall and built like oversized construction workers. Vinny himself was built, but he was no match for the two men together, that was for sure. But nobody, especially someone like Vinny allows himself to be abducted easily. He put up a fight, struggling like a madman, but to no avail. He struggled some more in Cleeve's grasp as the big man walked and tottered him toward the back of the van. Otis walked ahead of them and opened the back doors. Vinny seethed, "Fucking bastards!!" at the two men, asking them what the hell they wanted, asking what in all hell was going on here."

"And you mean to say that no one saw what was going on, a guy being kidnapped right off the street while he was on his way to work?" Don asked me in disbelief.

"No one," I replied. "Remember, it was five AM. The area was deserted."

"Poor Vinny," Don said. "What did they do to him?"

"I'm getting to that," I responded. "Let me continue. Otis climbed up into the back of the van. Cleeve swung Vinny's legs up and into the van and Otis grabbed Vinny by the ankles. Together, the two men hoisted Vinny into the back of the van. Vinny, realizing at that moment what the hell was going on roared at the top of his lungs, "Fuck, I-I'm bein' kidnapped!!" yelping and screaming in terror, "Help me!! *Oh God, someone, please help me!!!"*

"Yell all you want handsome guy," Otis said teasingly and mockingly to Vinny. "No one is going to come. This is New York after all."

"Fuckers!!" Vinny panted as they hoisted him bodily into the van, demanding that they put him the fuck down. "And then they did put him down, on a cot that was bolted to the floor of the van. Before Vinny knew what the fuck was happening he was tightly strapped down to the cot. Otis crammed a rag in Vinny's mouth, gagging him and tied a rope over the rag, jamming it firmly in place. Vinny struggled again like crazy, this time to pull free of the binding straps, but it was impossible. *He was trapped.* Cleeve and Otis hopped out of the van, closing and locking the doors behind them."

The only sounds our petrified buddy was able to make at that point were sounds like "MMMMMFFFF!!!" as he screamed into the gag," I went on. "Then, the van started moving and Vinny felt a wave of terror like nothing he had ever felt before in his life literally wash over him."

Before continuing I took a few sips of my club soda.

"My God, poor Vinny," Don whispered, looking at me nearly pale faced.

"Vinny broke out in a sweat as the van pulled away, leaving no trace that he had ever been there that morning, except for his attaché case laying in the street," I said, continuing. "Vinny was able to hear the two men up front in the van, they were laughing and congratulating themselves on a great fucking catch. Vinny was totally befuddled. A great fucking catch? The poor guy had no clue as to WHY he had been kidnapped."

"Where did they take him?" Don asked, looking terror stricken himself.

"I really don't know for sure," I replied. "Vinny told me that that blindfolded him before taking him out of the van. And there were no windows in the back of the van. Vinny estimated that they had driven for about an hour and a half or so.

When they'd reached their destination the van stopped in a garage of some sort. Vinny said he figured it was a garage they had rolled into because he heard the sound of a metal door being rolled up and then down again. Cleeve and Otis stepped up into the back of the van and looked down at their helpless prisoner. Vinny said that there was a look of outright hunger in the two men's eyes and he shivered involuntarily in fear under the tight and binding straps. Otis leaned down and tied a white cloth blindfold over Vinny's eyes and then he and Cleeve undid the straps holding our buddy to the cot. Then, holding Vinny by his arms in vise-like grips they walked him gagged and blindfolded into the house they had brought him to. Vinny was of course struggling and kicking his legs like mad, trying to pull free of those vise-like grips, but it was impossible. The two men were as strong as bulls and just as big."

"C'mon handsome guy, stop your stupid struggling!!" Cleeve shouted meanly at Vinny. "You ain't goin' no-fucking-where till we're done with you!" I said.

"Vinny made sounds like "RRRMMMFFF", roaring into his gag, knowing all too well what these two guys would want with a handsome dude like him," I went on. "They brought our buddy down a flight of stairs into a basement, or, more like a dungeon of sorts. Once they were down there Otis yanked Vinny's blindfold off him and Vinny saw that the basement was chock filled with all sorts of erotic devices, devices of sexual torture to be exact. He looked around in disbelief and as he did Otis took the gag out of the poor captured guy's mouth. The first thing Vinny said was, "Oh shit guys, I honestly think you have the wrong man, gulping his words out, stuttering a bit. I'm, I'm really not into all this shit, if you know what I mean. He looked desperately at the two men for a response, but all they did was laugh hysterically. Then, to Vinny's further shock and astonishment they pulled his suit jacket off him and threw it on the floor. Next, they pulled our buddy's tie off him and began unbuttoning his crisp white shirt."

Before continuing I again sipped my club soda…

"H-hey!!!" Vinny yelled as he was literally being stripped. "What the fuck do you think you're doing? This is going too far now!!!" Vinny managed to pull away from the two men and stood there shaking in his shoes as he looked at Cleeve and Otis as threateningly as possible."

Don and Robert had gone silent as mice at this point…

"Vinny buttoned his shirt back up and looked at the two men," I said. "He told them to give him his jacket and tie, said that he would walk out of there, wherever there was, and that he would forget that this ever happened, holding up a trembling finger as he spoke. The two men looked at each other, laughed and guffawed insanely and simply grabbed poor Vinny again. This time they proceeded to literally rip and tear his shirt off him and throw the tatters of it to the floor."

"Goddamn it all!!" Vinny seethed angrily as one of his most expensive dress shirts was shredded from his body," I said.

"Mmm, nice chest," Cleeve commented, I went on almost breathlessly now, as he ran and rubbed a big paw-like hand over Vinny's chest, saying how he liked our buddy's tits too. Otis then pinched one of Vinny's nipples hard and Vinny yelped in pain. Then, the two men forced Vinny over a table. On top of the table there were shackles at each corner. They slumped him over the table on his stomach till Vinny's feet were just about dangling off the floor. They then locked Vinny's wrists in the shackles and proceeded to finish undressing him. The two men stepped behind our buddy and squatting down they pulled Vinny's shoes off his feet and then pulled his suit pants down and off him. Vinny swore at them like a sailor who hasn't gotten laid in months, but they simply ignored him and ran their mangy hands over his calves, ass and feet, prodding his asshole, squeezing his socked calves and feet and kneading his ass cheeks as well. Vinny said he felt totally humiliated and worse that he was utterly helpless to stop them. Cleeve and Otis stood up behind Vinny and Otis tore the back of Vinny's white briefs off him, exposing his somewhat hairy butt.

"Man oh man, I am getting hot just hearing this shit now," Don said. "I mean, okay, I feel bad and all that for Vinny, but I can't deny that the image of hunky Vinny all bound up and being stripped just really gets me in the cock Chris."

"Me too man, me too," Robert agreed.

"Let me continue," I said to them, not wanting to lose my train of thought. "Vinny was now wearing just his torn white briefs and gray and black checkered dress socks. Now you know why Vinny told me what kind of socks he wore that day. He was still swearing like a sailor as the two men pulled his muscular legs apart, spreading him out, and exposing his bunghole. Then, the two men squatted and hunkered down behind Vinny and began viciously and hungrily taking turns eating his hole. Their tongues darted deeply into his gaping hole, swirled around in there and they even sucked like crazy on his ass walls, sending chills like you can't believe through our shackled and spread out buddy. They squeezed Vinny's ass cheeks hard and kneaded them as they lapped like two mangy mongrels in and out of his hole, getting it prepped for what they had in mind. Vinny, being the macho and studly guy he is ranted and seethed things like, "Fucking perverts, eating my damned mangy hole!!" at them, looking over his shoulder down at them and screaming "AAAARRRRHHH GAWDS" at the sight of the two men munching at his most private opening."

Don and Robert looked at me in total bewilderment at that point...

"They ate, licked and sucked at Vinny's hole like two animals in heat, taking turns at it," I said, not losing a beat in the story I was relating. "By the time they stopped the sides of Vinny's hole were sore to the touch, that's how much they had devoured it. Now I know as well as you guys that having your hole eaten can be very stimulating, but in this case it was anything but stimulating. But the two men, Cleeve and Otis, didn't stop the torment there. No fucking way, they had a lot more in mind for Vinny before the day was over. They prodded our buddy's moist hole with their fingers, sticking two and three fingers in there at a time, preparing him.

Vinny gasped and reeled and his head spun as he was finger fucked and then the two men resumed eating his hole, taking turns again, torturing it with the tips of their tongues and even nipping at it as well, driving the poor guy crazy."

"Was uh, was Vinny's dick hard in his briefs?" Don asked me.

"Yes, Vinny had to admit to himself that he was very aroused, very hard and even throbbing in his briefs," I replied. "Still, he was furious at being raped this way. The two men then stood up and slowly got undressed down to their white sweat socks. Vinny whimpered things like, "Oh no, no," knowing full well what was next."

"Did Cleeve and Otis have big dicks?" Robert asked me.

"Enormous," I responded. "When Vinny saw their huge, fat, hard cocks he gulped twice in mortal terror. His hole had never accommodated such big pieces of meat before. He begged them futilely, nearly crying out the word, *"No,"* over and over again. Cleeve mocked Vinny and asked him, "Whatsamatter handsome guy, you a virgin or something?" as he stepped behind our buddy, his huge dick hard, rigid and ready. Vinny saw that there was no way out so he simply blubbered, "N-no, just that…" but Cleeve cut him off in mid-sentence by saying, "Never seen such big fucking cocks before huh? Well, get ready you handsome fuck, because this is going to be like nothing you've ever felt before." Cleeve pushed the tip of his huge cock head against Vinny's hole and slid it in halfway. Vinny's breath caught in his throat with just the first half of Cleeve's beefy dick in his hole. Vinny cried out in mortal pain, swearing at Cleeve, calling him a bastard and other choice words that popped into his head."

Otis teased Vinny verbally by saying to Cleeve, "His hole sure does taste good huh Cleeve?" I said as he licked and smacked his lips together. Cleeve agreed and added, "But now we'll get it tasting even better when we cum in there. As he spoke Cleeve thrust the rest of his enormous manhood into Vinny's hole. This time when Vinny screamed his voice reached a high crescendo that even he never knew he could hit. Cleeve meanly gyrated his hips seductively as he thrust in and out of our buddy's hole, torturing the guy, spearing him. He slapped Vinny's ass cheeks as he mercilessly fucked him like crazy. Vinny was swearing, crying and roaring in pain all at the same time. When Cleeve came he shot his giant load of sperm into Vinny's hole, drenching it. He continued thrusting till his dick went soft and then it slowly slipped out. Cleeve told Otis it was his turn."

"Holy shit!!" Don gasped. "You have got to be kidding. You mean, right after Cleeve finished fucking Vinny Otis rammed his tool in him?"

"Less than a few seconds later," I replied, looking at Don without smiling. "Otis stepped behind Vinny, and like Cleeve had done, pressed the tip of his big man tool against Vinny's wet hole. Vinny whimpered and pleaded things like, "Please man, no," to Otis' deaf ears. Otis slowly pushed his fat dick into Vinny's hole, slapping his ass cheeks hard.

Vinny then swore revenge of the worst kind, telling the two men that he would kill them for what they were doing to him. In reply the two men laughed and Otis rammed his dick further and further into Vinny's poor hole. At that point Vinny screamed in utter agony, his head falling to the table. With his teeth clenched he cried out in pain, big tears flowing down his cheeks."

"My God, the poor guy," Robert whispered.

"Vinny balled his shackled hands into tight fists as Otis thrust in and out of his hole like mad," I said. "Our buddy was sweating profusely by now. Cleeve mockingly told him that if he would relax it would be a lot easier for him. But of course who could relax under *those* circumstances? I mean, he'd been kidnapped and now he was being raped. A short while later Otis shot his load into Vinny's hole, grunting, swearing like a marine and slapping the fuck out of Vinny's ass cheeks till they shone red."

"OH YEAH, that was good Cleeve," Otis said breathlessly as his fat dick slipped out of Vinny's hole." I said. "Cleeve agreed and said that he bet it was, him holding his hard dick in hand and at the ready. He smiled evilly and said he hoped that the handsome guy was ready for round two. When Vinny craned his neck and saw that Cleeve was again hard as steel he screeched wildly, "SHIT NO!!! NO!!!" as Cleeve stepped behind him for a second time. Vinny could not believe it and all he could scream was, "You, you fucking bastard!! Hard again already???"

"But then, Vinny cried out in agony all over again as Cleeve's hard dick rammed mightily into his hole," I said, continuing the story. "Vinny could not even utter words at this point. He had all to do just to keep breathing normally. His head was spinning and he felt as if he was going to pass out. It took Cleeve a little while longer to shoot his load this time. And when he did he panted and grunted things like, "Oh yeah, fucking hot hole you have handsome guy!! I could fuck you all day and night!! And all Vinny could do in response to that threat was scream some more in pain. Cleeve slapped Vinny's ass cheeks hard as he fucked him and fucked him and fucked him some more. Then, he shot a load into Vinny's already sopping wet hole, swearing and cursing breathlessly as he came like a bandit into Vinny's crevice. Then, Cleeve said, "Otis my man, I think this hole is ready for eatin' again. Vinny lifted his head and roared, "PERVERTS!!!" as Cleeve's dick slid again out of his hole."

"They ripped Vinny's briefs off him and squatted behind him again, their tongues eager and their mouths hungry now for his wet and warmed up hole," I continued, speaking a tad slower at that point. "They began taking turns again lapping and licking at Vinny's now stretched hole, licking their cum out of it like crazy, reclaiming in a way what was theirs. Vinny moaned and groaned miserably as his hole was victimized by their tongues. But Vinny's dick had betrayed him. It was hard as a rock, and it didn't take long for the two men to notice this fact. Otis reached under Vinny's crotch and grabbed the poor guy's hard dick. He pulled it back further, under Vinny's ass crack. Vinny screamed out, "ACCCCCC!!! Ea-easy with my dick you fucker!!"

Laughing, Otis said, "Hey Cleeve, look at this hard piece of beef of his."

And look Cleeve did, very intensely at our buddy's erection. Cleeve then stated, "Looks good enough to eat too. You can go first this time Otis my man." And with that Otis tongued Vinny's dick hole, opening it as he poked it, opening it as wide as possible, and teasing the fuck out of it with the tip of his tongue, Vinny cried out first in pain, but then took a breath of outright man's passion as Otis greedily gobbled our buddy's meat into his mouth and began sucking it…HARD."

"OOOHHHH yeah, eat my dick you bastard!!" Vinny swore like a marine, still looking over his shoulder at his captors I said. "Fucking gulp down my jazzy jazz when I cum." Vinny clenched his teeth again and pumped his dick in and out of Otis' mouth."

"Does Vinny have a big dick?" Don asked me curiously and anxiously. "I've always wondered."

"Yeah, pretty big," I said to Don. "Not too long, but nice and fat and beefy. So, Otis sucked our buddy like crazy, like his life depended on it, and when Vinny shot his load the guy did swallow his jazz, every fucking drop of it. Vinny had shot a load big enough to choke a horse, a load made so big and potent mostly by fear. When Otis was done gulping down Vinny's juices he let his dick slip slowly out of his mouth and then Cleeve took his turn. He instantly gobbled Vinny's sensitive feeling and slimy dick into his mouth, not even giving it a chance to go soft. Vinny's eyes crossed in his head and he screamed, *"ohhhhh no, no you fucker!"* utter disbelief engulfing him. *"Not again so fucking soon!! I'm still sensitive man!!!"*

"Otis stood there chuckling as poor Vinny was milked like a cow," I said, shaking my head sadly. "But, believe it or not a little while later Vinny did shoot a second load, not as powerful and as hefty as the first one was, but enough for that bastard Cleeve to swallow and tease Vinny's cock as he did so. Vinny gasped breathlessly and shook and trembled on the table as Cleeve forcefully sucked and suckled every possible drop out of our buddy's piss slit. Then, Vinny's dick hung freely behind his legs as Otis stepped behind him, his hard dick in his hand."

"No, oh fucking no!!" Vinny cried at Otis, I said. "Not after I just shot two fucking creamy and over the top loads!!!"

"But then, Vinny screamed in total agony as Otis rammed his hard fat dick into his hole a second time. Now I don't know about you guys, but after I've cum my asshole is more than sensitive, it's downright off limits to any dick. Vinny had shot two loads, so you can just imagine how fucking sensitive his bunghole was at that moment." Don and Robert nodded their agreement.

"His hole had to be more than sensitive Chris," Don said to me in amazement. "After being fucked like that AND eaten and then fucked again it had to be totally sore to the touch. God, the poor guy."

"I would think so too," I agreed and went on. "But there's more to this story. Can you two handle it? You're both starting to look a little peeked."

"I can take it," Robert practically whispered.

"Me too," Don said. "Please continue."

They were totally enthralled. Even though what I was telling them was a horror story of sorts, they were definitely intrigued. I suppose they were wondering how they would handle it if what happened to Vinny happened to them.

"Okay, here goes," I said to them. "Otis came a second time, shooting his load in Vinny's poor hole. He and Cleeve licked all that cum out of Vinny's hole as well, further adding to the torment of his sore rectal opening. Then, they undid the shackles on Vinny's wrists, pulled him to his feet and held him up and steady by his upper muscular arms. Vinny was listless and groggy as they ran their hands over his sweaty muscular body and squeezed and kneaded his hot ass cheeks."

"Feelin' good handsome guy?" Cleeve asked Vinny mockingly as he caressed his chest and teased his nipples."

"All Vinny was able to mumble was, *"F-f-fucking bastards you two are,"* I said. "He barely croaked out the words. Cleeve then told our buddy that that was just the warm up, speaking directly into Vinny's ear, licking his earlobe as he spoke. Cleeve said, "The next round is coming up." Vinny looked from side to side at his captors in disbelief. How much more did they expect him to take? And how much more could they possibly dish out and Vinny wondered how much energy these two sick fucks could have. All these questions raced through Vinny's mind. And the poor guy was about to find out. The two men lifted our buddy by his upper arms and literally carried him over to a wooden post, which was situated in the center of the room...

(Part 2)

"Vinny found himself tied to the post with his wrists behind him, sort of the way that that porn star Jimmy Dean was roped to the post in that porno flick "Ranch Slave Trainee," I said to Don and Robert after having refilled their glasses with club soda. "Vinny's socked feet were also tied securely to the post. He stood there helplessly and immobilized as Cleeve and Otis circled him a few times. They touched him everywhere, squeezed his nipples hard squeezed his dick and even his big juicy balls. They taunted him like crazy, telling him that they were considering not letting him go at all and keeping him forever as their sex slave. Vinny glared up at the ceiling, clenched his teeth and closed his eyes tight to stop the tears of fear from falling again. Instead Vinny found the strength to rant at them in anger, saying things like, "You fuckers!! You two will pay for this, *for all of it! I will personally see to that!!*"

"Then, Cleeve and Otis each took one of Vinny's nipples into their mouth and began working them hard," I said. "They sucked, bit and nipped and even kissed Vinny's big brown nipples, running their fingers through the mat of hair on Vinny's big muscular chest at the same time. Vinny crooned in somewhat ecstasy and pain. His dick began to get hard again, a fact that even he found hard to believe. Cleeve and Otis slurped on Vinny's nipples like two hungry nursing babies. When it did become painful Vinny pushed his chest out, causing the two men to eat his tits even more."

"AAARRGGGHHH, bastards, fucking kidnappers!!" Vinny swore. "You two will go to jail for this!!"

"The two men simply ignored their captive and sucked heartily on his nipples, they sucked Vinny's nipples till they were sore, red and erect beyond reason," I said. "They finally stopped, licking around and around Vinny's muscular chest a bit, stroking his sides with the palms of their hands, cupping his sexy ass cheeks in their big hands and squeezing them hard."

"Okay Otis, I think his tits are sore enough now," Cleeve said then, I went on. "And you know what that means. Otis said that he sure did know what that meant. He eagerly dashed over to a shelf on which were various storage boxes. Otis opened one of the small boxes and took out a pair of sharp looking tit clamps. When Vinny saw the clamps he begged the two men not to clamp his tits, especially since they were so fucking sore and swollen. But, as I'm sure you've already guessed

Otis snapped the tit clamps tightly onto poor Vinny's nipples. Vinny could not hold back the tears now as the clamps bit unforgivingly into the tender flesh of his sore nipples. He stood there crying helplessly, swearing and cursing at the two men who had abducted him. But then, to his astonishment, Otis knelt down in front of him and slurped Vinny's dick into his mouth."

"OHHHH GAWD, you bastard, sucking my damned meat again," Vinny gasped as Otis feasted heartily and most greedily on his big meat stick. "Fucking torturing me and driving me wild at the same time."

"As Otis sucked Vinny's dick Cleeve stepped next to him, turned Vinny's face to him and kissed Vinny tenderly on the mouth, sucking Vinny's tongue like it was a dick," I said, almost breathless myself now. "Vinny responded to Cleeve's kiss only because he didn't want to anger the big guy. As Cleeve kissed him and Otis sucked his dick Vinny momentarily forgot about the pain that his nipples were in."

"Did Vinny shoot a third load?" Robert asked me.

"No, not at that moment," I replied. "Otis only sucked Vinny to get him good and hard so he could snap a cock ring onto the poor guy's cock and balls, which he did, once Vinny was again hard and throbbing."

"Ouch," Don said, placing a hand over his crotch and grimacing.

"Vinny's words exactly," I replied agreeably. "Cleeve stopped kissing our buddy and then he and Otis watched as Vinny writhed in total agony while tied to that post, his nipples clamped and a tight, tight cock ring hugging his cock and balls."

"Good choice eh Otis my man?" Cleeve asked his buddy and Otis said, "Damn good choice, saying it most enthusiastically.

"Vinny seethed angrily against the post and spat at the two men, not reaching either of them however," I went on with the story. "The two men laughed and cackled at him. They, they stepped over to Vinny, stood on either side of him and began slapping his flat stomach area hard with the palms of their hands. Vinny yelped at the stinging blows, which slowly turned into light punches and then harder ones. Vinny was unable to double over in pain because of the position he was tied in so he was forced to take the blows the hard way. Cleeve and Otis knocked the wind out of him till poor Vinny's head hung down limply. Vinny drooled involuntarily over his chest, trying desperately to catch his breath."

"Then, a short while later Cleeve said, "Let's get those clamps and cock ring off him," saying it with total authority I said to Don and Robert. "I want to get started on spanking his butt."

"Otis hooted happily, "All right man!!" and clapped his meaty hands together," I said. "Looking at Vinny Otis said, "Handsome guy, we have various devices that we can use to redden that hot butt of yours."

"Vinny looked away from Otis in outright misery," I said sadly. "After all they had done to him already now they were going to spank him too."

"What kind of devices did they use to spank him with?" Robert asked me.

"I'll get to that," I said. "Don't rush this. "Anyhow, Vinny soon found himself over Cleeve's knees with his hands cuffed in front of himself. His butt was directly over Cleeve's lap, a ready target. The tit clamps and cock ring were off him. Cleeve was holding a round leather paddle in his hand; rubbing it tauntingly over and over Vinny's melon shaped butt cheeks as Otis stood by with a pair of dice in his hands. Cleeve then said, "Okay handsome guy, its spanking time for you," still rubbing the paddle over Vinny's exquisite butt cheeks and chuckling meanly at the same time. Cleeve then added, "Maybe this will clear up that attitude of yours."

"Fucker!!" Vinny screamed and pressed his socked feet hard against the floor.

"Now, the rules," Cleeve said. "Otis and I will spank you, three rounds each at a time. A roll of a pair of dice will determine how many swats this hot ass of yours will receive."

"I-I can take it you bastard!!" Vinny roared. "Just you watch and fucking see!"

"Cleeve smiled at Otis and asked him if he should tell Vinny the rest of the rules," I said. "Otis said that he should."

"If Otis rolls double digits on the dice you will receive double the amount of swats of that number," Cleeve explained, squeezing one of Vinny's butt cheeks as he spoke. "Damn, but you have a hot ass. So, let's say Otis rolls two fives. Rather than ten swats with this paddle you'll receive twenty, *hard ones.*"

"Vinny looked up at Otis who was standing there smiling mockingly down at him," I said to Don and Robert. "Otis was flipping the dice from hand to hand, ready for Cleeve's word so he could begin"

"You fucking sadistic and sick bastards!!" Vinny yelled and lowered his head again.

"Roll the dice Otis," Cleeve said.

"Gladly," Otis replied and shook up the dice in his hands.

"Otis threw the dice on a table and all the men saw that he had rolled a five and a two," I told Don and Robert.

"Seven!!" Cleeve said and raised the paddle. "A good and lucky number to start off with."

"Cleeve brought the paddle down hard on Vinny's butt cheeks," I said and sipped my soda. "Poor Vinny yelped in pain, but swore through clenched teeth that he would be able to take it. Cleeve swatted his butt a second and third time, harder. Vinny yelped in pain after each swat and Cleeve paddled him a fourth and then a fifth time."

"AYYYYYYYY!!!!" Vinny roared and squirmed on Cleeve's lap as Cleeve brought the paddle down a sixth time. "BASTARD!!!"

"The seventh swat was the hardest and Vinny's butt was already turning red," I said. "Then, Cleeve told Otis to roll the dice."

"Judging from the expression on your face I get the feeling that the news from the dice wasn't good," Don said to me.

"It wasn't," I replied sadly. "Otis rolled two sixes. When Vinny saw the double sixes his breath caught in his throat. Cleeve and Otis cackled happily and more mockingly.

"Oh fuck, oh fuck," Vinny muttered. "Shit, shit, SHIT!!!!"

"Whooooo boy, you are in for it now handsome guy!!" Cleeve said loudly and meanly. "Twenty-four hard ones coming right the fuck up!! And just think, we're just getting started here."

"Give it to him good Cleeve," Otis encouraged his deranged buddy. "I want to hear him scream."

"Handsome guy, I want you to count each swat that I give you," Cleeve said to Vinny and meanly stuck a finger up Vinny's ass.

"YOWWWWW!!" Vinny yelped in surprise.

"Is that clear?" Cleeve asked him.

"Yeah, yeah, perfectly clear man," Vinny responded.

Cleeve pulled his finger out of Vinny's hole and raised the paddle," I said. "He began spanking our buddy again."

"OWWWWW, ONE!!" Vinny roared.

SWAT

"Two!!" Vinny yelled in pain.

SWAT SWAT SWAT

"YOWWWCCCHHHH!!!! Three, four, OWWWWWWW, five!!!" Vinny yelled through clenched teeth. "DAMN IT!!"

Vinny balled his hands into a big fist and squeezed his eyes shut tight as Cleeve raised the paddle," I went on.

SWAT SWAT SWAT

"Six, OWWWWWWW, seven you bastard!!" Vinny screeched. "Eight, damn my poor ass!!!"

Cleeve brought the paddle down harder and harder on Vinny's reddening butt," I said. "Tears welled up in Vinny's eyes as the big man tortured him and tortured him.

SWAT SWAT SWAT

"Nine, ten, eleven, owwwwwwwwww!!!" Vinny cried. "T-twelve!!

"Hey handsome guy, I thought you said you could take it," Otis teased Vinny. "Are those tears I see in your eyes?"

"Fucker!!" Vinny responded loudly, spittle flying from his mouth. "Mock me all you want, *but I can take this!!* And you fucking kidnappers will pay!!"

"Cleeve swatted Vinny's butt hard four more times to shut him up," I said.

"YOWWWWWWCCCHHHH!!!! Thirteen, fourteen, fifteen, sixteen...*owwwwwwww!!!*" Vinny cried now in a high-pitched tone of voice.

SWAT SWAT SWAT

"Seventeen, eighteen, *nineteen,"* Vinny squealed.

"By now Vinny's butt was a most definite shade of dark red I might add," I said. "But Vinny is strong and tough and he continued counting off the swats that Cleeve was giving him. Each swat was harder and worse than the one before. This wasn't some erotic spanking scene being played out...this was outright sadism that Vinny was suffering."

"Poor fucking guy," Robert said softly. "I would have been begging them to stop after five damn swats from a leather paddle. That shit must more than hurt, that has to fucking sting and burn."

"Vinny told me that he felt as if his ass was on fire," I said to Robert. "Let me go on. Cleeve swatted Vinny's butt the final five times, making it a total of twenty-four swats for that round. Vinny cried out each number, choking and sobbing. When it was done Cleeve rubbed

Vinny's wounded ass with the palm of his hand. That ass was warm to the touch and would soon be even warmer."

"Tough guy, you are a handsome fucking guy," Cleeve said to Vinny soothingly. "But we're not done yet. We still have a way to go."

"Pl-please man, no more, no more," Vinny sobbed as he shook like a leaf on Cleeve's lap.

"Cleeve and Otis looked at each other and smiled," I said, not heeding Vinny's cries at all. "Cleeve told Otis to shake up the dice and roll 'em."

"No, NO!!!" Vinny cried as Cleeve held him tight on his lap.

"Handsome guy, you still have a lot of spanking to endure, so if I were you I would save my strength and shut the fuck up," Cleeve said and gave Vinny's butt two hard bonus swats with the leather paddle.

"OWWWWWWW!!!" Vinny cried.

"I'll bet his daddy never spanked him this hard," Otis said and shook up the dice.

"My father was a good man!!" Vinny ranted. "He would never have tortured me this way!!"

"Oh no?" Cleeve asked. "How would he have tortured you?"

"The two men laughed meanly at Cleeve's joke," I said.

"Roll the dice," Cleeve then said to Otis. "Otis dropped the dice on the table and all three of the men saw that he had rolled a four and a one."

"Five hard ones," Otis announced. "And then it's my turn to work on those hot butt cheeks of yours handsome guy."

"Cleeve raised the paddle and brought it down hard on Vinny's red ass cheeks five times very quickly and very, VERY, intensely," I said. "He only paddled him five times that time but to Vinny it felt more like twenty-five times, that's how hard Cleeve whacked him. The sounds of the paddle connecting with flesh echoed loudly in the room. When he was done Cleeve pushed Vinny off his lap to his feet. Vinny stood there with his hands cuffed in front of him, wearing just his gray and black checkered socks, sobbing loudly. His cock, to his utter disbelief was hard and throbbing fiercely. He looked down at Cleeve who was still sitting on the chair and holding his paddle."

"Y-you fucking monster!!" Vinny choked. "This is inhuman!!!"

Cleeve stood up and he and Otis stepped close to Vinny," I said, looking intently at Don and Robert. "They ordered Vinny to raise his arms up over his head and to hold them there. Being in no position to argue Vinny did as he was told. The two men began licking and sucking Vinny's sweaty armpits, sucking the sweat and raunch out of them like crazy and licking his raunchy armpit hair as well."

"Now that sounds kinky but good," Don commented. "I've never had someone lick my armpits for me."

"Neither have I," Robert added.

"Neither had Vinny," I responded. "He said that for the moment it did feel good at that, but at the same time he knew that it was only a brief reprieve before the two burly men started in torturing him again. He simply stood there with his muscular arms over his head as the two men licked heartily at his stinking pits. And I'm sure that picturing Vinny in that position is enough to get you two going."

"Man, I am so fucking hot right now that you would not believe it," Robert said. "I mean, the poor guy, I'm not saying that what they did to him is right, *but oh man.*"

"I know what you mean," I said slowly. "When Vinny told me all this I had to admit that it was driving me crazy as well. A fucking muscle guy like Vinny being thoroughly worked over *is* most gay guy's fantasy. Now, on with the story. Cleeve and Otis stopped licking Vinny's armpits. A few seconds later Vinny found himself over Otis' knees with his already red butt over the guy's lap. Vinny's butt was going to be turned even redder now because Otis was holding a large round hairbrush in his hand. Cleeve stood by with the dice in his hand."

"Oh boy, are you going to scream now handsome guy," Otis said, rubbing the hairbrush over Vinny's backside. "This shit is going to sting like you would not believe. Cleeve, roll the dice if you would."

"Gladly," Cleeve responded and shook up the dice.

"No, no, please no," Vinny whimpered helplessly.

"Cleeve threw the dice down on the table and the numbers were a four and a five," I said. "Otis raised the hairbrush and brought it down hard on Vinny's butt. Vinny screeched in pain as the bristles stung his rear end. Then, over and over Otis whacked Vinny's butt hard. At that point Vinny was screaming, crying and trembling in agony as Otis whacked his poor butt nine hard times with the hairbrush. When Otis stopped, after having gotten to the ninth swat, he ran his hand tenderly over Vinny's wounded butt cheeks."

"Fucking hot enough to fry an egg on," Otis said to Cleeve and pinched Vinny's RED butt a few times.

"I'll roll the dice again," Cleeve said eagerly and Vinny thundered, "NO, NO, OH GAWDS NO!!!" I said. "Vinny was practically hoarse by then.

"P-PLEASE…enough of this already man!!" Vinny beseeched Cleeve.

"But of course Cleeve ignored Vinny and shook up the dice," I said sadly. "Vinny lowered his head and looked down at the floor as Cleeve threw the dice on the table. He had rolled a six and a two. Otis wasted no time. He brought the hairbrush down on Vinny's butt, HARD. Vinny was beyond screaming now. He simply whimpered as Otis feverishly beat his butt with the hairbrush."

"He probably felt like dying at that point," Don said, looking at me blankly.

"Not really," I replied. "Remember, Vinny is a tough and strong fucking guy, a real bull. More than anything he was pissed the fuck off at what was being done to him. But what he did next surprised even him."

"What the fuck did Vinny do?" Robert asked me.

"Well, as Otis was giving Vinny his eight swats with the hairbrush Vinny began licking Otis' feet, lapping at the smelly sweat socks he was wearing," I said. "Vinny's tears landed on Otis' socks and he watched in awe as our buddy licked and seemed to be even worshipping his big feet. He squeezed Vinny's butt as the captured guy licked his feet more and more."

"Look at this shit, will you Cleeve?" Otis asked his buddy. "He's fucking licking my damned feet man!"

"So I see," Cleeve replied with a wicked looking smile on his face.

"The two men watched as Vinny wrapped his cuffed hands around Otis' ankles and continued working his feet with his tongue," I said. "Vinny even sucked at Otis' socked toes."

"They had beaten down his resolve after all," Don commented.

"I don't think so," I said, disagreeing with Don. "*I think* that Vinny was just trying to buy some time. He had already suffered fifty-three hard swats to his ass. Remember, Otis still had another round of spanking to go. And then Cleeve was going to have another go at Vinny's butt."

"Shit, the poor fucking guy," Don whispered.

"Do you want me to continue or have you heard enough at this point?" I asked my two friends.

"Go on," Robert begged. "I have to know how it turns out."

"Okay," I said. "As Vinny was licking Otis' feet Otis told Cleeve to roll the dice. Vinny looked up in disbelief, begging Cleeve not to roll the dice. Tears streamed out of Vinny's eyes in rivers. Cleeve rolled the dice, rolling double fours. He and Otis laughed meanly and hysterically. Vinny sobbed as he lay helplessly over Otis' knees."

"Double fours," Robert said very sadly. "That meant he was going to get sixteen more swats with that damned hairbrush."

"Unfortunately that's right," I said to Robert.

"Didn't those two monsters show Vinny any mercy at all?" Don asked me angrily.

"None whatsoever," I responded. "Now, Otis raised the hairbrush and brought it down hard on Vinny's sore, sore butt, over and over. He made Vinny count each pummeling blow, adding to the torment by swatting his butt harder and harder with each one. "Vinny counted, sobbed uncontrollably and swore like a captured marine all at the same time.

When Otis was done poor Vinny's butt was more than red and crimson; it had large welts all over it. Both men had each gone three rounds of spanking our buddy intensely with the leather paddle and then the hairbrush. And yet *they still weren't done.*"

"Sixty-nine times they had whapped and whipped the guy's butt and that still wasn't enough?" Robert asked me, a look of outright astonishment on his face. "How much more did they want to give him? How much more could Vinny take?"

"They wanted to spank him with the backs of their hands this time," I said to Robert. "One round each…"

"That's what they decided?" Don asked.

"Yes, it's what Cleeve decided," I said. "Obviously it was Cleeve who was in charge. They stood Vinny up on his socked feet and together they rubbed handfuls of aloe lotion all over his much wounded butt cheeks. That wasn't to be merciful; rather it was to prevent bleeding. Chills sped through Vinny's muscular body as Cleeve and Otis rubbed and squeezed his butt cheeks as they applied the lotion most liberally. Then, Cleeve sat down and Otis helped Vinny down onto his lap. By now Vinny was in a daze and his head was spinning. Otis picked up the dice, he shook them up and threw them on the table."

"A six and a one," Otis announced.

"Seven good hard whacks coming up handsome guy," Cleeve said, rubbing and rubbing Vinny's greasy butt. "God, but you have a great piece of ass."

"S-seven," Vinny whispered pitifully.

"Cleeve raised his hand and brought it down hard on Vinny's butt," I said. "Aloe cream flew into the air from Vinny's butt cheeks.

"YOWWWWWW!!!" Vinny screamed, coming quickly out of his daze.

"Cleeve was a strong mother fucker," I said. "He put everything he had into those whacks he gave Vinny with the back of his hand. Each whack was harder and worse than the one before. By the time he got to the fourth whack Vinny was begging him to stop."

"But he didn't," Don whispered.

"Nope, he just whaled into poor Vinny like there was no tomorrow," I replied sadly. "When Cleeve was done Vinny found himself over Otis' knees again, ready for yet *more spanking.* Vinny lay docilely over Otis' knees as Cleeve rolled the dice. This time the numbers were a four and a two."

"At least it wasn't doubles," Robert said. "My damn butt is hurting just listening to this shit."

"Yeah, a small number, a six," I said to Robert. "But at that point, for Vinny, even a one would have been torture. Otis raised his hand and brought it down hard and mercilessly on Vinny's much wounded butt. Our buddy screamed in more than agony as Otis pounded his butt cheeks with the back of his hand six times, hard. When it was finally over Otis pushed Vinny off his lap and to the floor on his knees. Vinny knelt there shaking and trembling and letting out gut wrenching sobs. The two men stood over him, looming like two monsters."

"Think we've adjusted his attitude Otis?" Cleeve asked his buddy.

"Sure as shit looks like we did Cleeve," Otis replied. "I don't hear any smart remarks coming out of that mouth of his now."

"Then let's fill that mouth of his," Cleeve suggested.

"All totaled they had given Vinny eighty-two hard swats to his hot butt," I said.

At that point I stopped and looked gravely at Don and Robert.

(Part 3)

"Why did you stop?" Robert asked me. "Is that it? Did they let Vinny go after all that spanking and shit?"

"No, they didn't let him go," I replied. "Not yet at least. I stopped because I think we need something a little stronger than soda at this point."

I stood up and went to the kitchen, leaving Don and Robert sitting in the living room.

"Man oh man, do you think you could endure eighty-two whacks to your ass, even if it were involved in an erotic scene?" Robert asked Don.

"No, I don't think I would even want to," Don replied. "Poor Vinny…"

I came back in with a can of Budweiser for each of us. I handed my friends one each and then settled back down, to continue my story.

"It was now close to afternoon," I went on. "Vinny had been there all morning at that point. He was by then very weak, very tired and more than very scared. But Cleeve and Otis were still not done with him, at least not yet. They had tied Vinny to an old-fashioned workout horse, which was mounted a few feet off the floor. His wrists were tied to the front of the thing and his feet were tied to the back, only his toes resting on the floor. Needless to say Vinny was in a very uncomfortable position, as you can imagine. Cleeve stood in front of our buddy, his big cock in Vinny's mouth. Vinny, obviously having no choice in the matter, sucked and slurped Cleeve's giant meat as Otis squatted behind him, licking and sucking Vinny's cock."

"Oh fuck yeah, after all that hard work spanking you it sure feels good to have my big cock sucked by you handsome guy," Cleeve said mockingly. "Yeah, eat my cock you cock sucker."

"Cleeve tweaked Vinny's nipples hard as the guy sucked him and sucked him," I said. "Cleeve's cock felt like it was alive in Vinny's mouth. He could feel it throbbing like mad. Then, Cleeve shot a giant load into Vinny's throat, forcing him to swallow every damned drop of it. Otis then took his turn as Cleeve sucked Vinny's cock from behind. Otis also shot his load into Vinny's mouth, forcing him to swallow his juices too. Vinny sputtered angrily around Otis' cock as the guy's juices slid down his throat. Vinny shot his load at the same time that Otis shot his and Cleeve had the pleasure of swallowing Vinny's sweet nectar."

Don and Robert sipped their beers, looking at me expectantly. No doubt the thought of swallowing Vinny's cum was driving them wild.

"They still weren't done torturing our friend," I said and took a gulp of my beer. "Vinny next found himself back on the table, slumped over it, his wrists shackled in front of him; his legs spread wide and a blindfold now tied over his eyes. Once again Cleeve and Otis were taking turns licking and sucking Vinny's asshole, squeezing his wounded ass cheeks at the same time, and just about all around making him nuts."

"Fuckers!!" Vinny ranted. "What's the point of all this? Fucking eating my damned hole all over again? Starting all over again??? Why the fucking fuck did you blindfold me??? *SHIT!!!!* "

"Looks like they hadn't adjusted Vinny's attitude after all," Robert commented happily. "Fucking tough guy was still fighting them, in his own way…"

"He sure was," I said agreeably. "They licked Vinny's hole till he was drenched with their mangy saliva back there. As they worked his hole they toyed with his socks, rolling them up and down and snapping the elastic in them. Then, when they removed Vinny's blindfold he saw five dildos lined up in front of him on the table. The dildos ranged in size from small to medium to fat and long. The last one didn't look to Vinny like it would be fitted into any human ass hole."

"*Shit,*" Vinny whispered and looked up at his two captors in disbelief.

"We'll start you off slow," Cleeve said, picking up the smallest of the dildos.

"Cleeve stepped behind Vinny and slowly inserted the smallest dildo in his hole," I said. "When it was in he began gyrating it around in there, thrusting it meanly in and out of Vinny's hole at the same time. Vinny felt one of the first sensations of pleasure since having been abducted that morning. His dick grew semi hard. Otis squatted in front of the guy, ran the tips of his fingers through Vinny's goatee and then kissed him hard on the lips."

"Mmmm…" Vinny and Otis crooned.

"Feels like you just gave me the kiss of death," Vinny whispered, as Cleeve yanked the first dildo out of his hole.

"Nah," Otis said and stroked Vinny's hair as Cleeve picked up the second dildo.

"The second dildo was a little larger than the first, but not by much," I said. "Cleeve slipped it into Vinny's hole pretty easily. As Cleeve fucked him with the second dildo Otis slid his tongue into Vinny's mouth, kissing him tenderly. Vinny responded in kind to Otis' kiss. At the same time Cleeve thrust the second dildo in and out of Vinny's hole, fucking him with it. Vinny continued kissing Otis as Otis stroked his hair. When Cleeve pulled the second dildo out of Vinny's hole he put it down and stuck three fingers into the guy's hole. Otis stopped kissing Vinny and our buddy moaned and groaned as Cleeve prodded his hole with three fingers.

"OOOOHHHHH fuck, yeahhhh," Vinny found himself crooning.

"He's pretty much stretched back here Otis," Cleeve said. "Looks like we'll have to get to the bigger dildos sooner than we thought."

"Allow me," Otis said, stepping next to Cleeve as Cleeve pulled his fingers out of Vinny's hole.

Otis picked up the third dildo, which was pretty thick and kind of long," I said. "Vinny turned his head and looked at Otis nervously as he began pushing the tip of the dildo into his gaping hole. Vinny cursed and swore softly under his breath as the dildo went in softly, inch by painful inch. Otis meanly twirled the dildo a little as it went deeper and deeper into Vinny's hole.

"OHHHHH you fucker," Vinny moaned and lay his head back down on the table. "I'll get you guys for this. I swear I will."

"Vinny's hole swallowed up half the dildo and then Otis pushed it all the way home, holding it by the end," I said. "Vinny thrust his hips back and forth as Otis fucked him with the third dildo. Cleeve squeezed and pinched Vinny's welted red butt cheeks as Otis went on and on fucking him with the dildo."

"Fun eh?" Cleeve asked Otis.

"Sure is Cleeve my man," Otis responded happily. "One of the best choices we've made in a while."

"From the sound of things they had done this sort of thing before to other men," Don said.

"Sure sounded that way," I agreed with him. "When Otis felt that Vinny had had enough of the third dildo he yanked it out and Cleeve picked up the fourth one, holding the thing in two hands."

"FUCK, you can't be thinking about shoving that thing inside me!!" Vinny choked. "For the love of God, look at the size of it!!"

"Yeah and just imagine how you're going to feel when we get to the fifth one," Cleeve said jokingly and pressed the tip of the dildo against Vinny's asshole.

"OH GODS, no, NO!!!" Vinny seethed through clenched teeth.

"He pulled angrily on the shackles around his wrists to no avail," I said. "There was of course no way that he could pull free. Vinny was forced to endure the agony as Cleeve pushed the fourth dildo slowly into his hole, twisting it around at the same time."

"ARRRGHHHH!!!!" Vinny cried loudly in pain "*Bastards!!!!*"

"Finally, the fourth dildo was all the way in," I said to Don and Robert. "Cleeve spanked Vinny's wounded butt cheeks as he laughed meanly, fucking Vinny horribly and mercilessly with the dildo. Vinny told me that it had felt like he was literally being ripped apart back there. His tears flowed down his cheeks, landing in his goatee. Otis kissed Vinny a few times on the mouth, but this time it did not alleviate the pain he was in. Cleeve tormented Vinny's hole for what seemed like hours with the dildo, twisting it around in there, thrusting it in and out and ramming it hard inside our buddy, making him scream in horrid pain, a pain that Vinny said no man should ever experience. Then, Cleeve pulled the dildo out all in one yank. The dildo came out with what sounded like a small pop. The two men laughed and laughed as Vinny lay there shaking and sobbing."

"Hey Cleeve, do you think that maybe we should gag him for this last one?" Otis asked Cleeve as he picked up the fifth and longest, thickest dildo from the table.

"Nah, I want to hear him scream for this one," Cleeve replied jokingly.

"OH God almighty, you really have got to be kidding now!!!" Vinny ranted miserably. "That thing is a monster-sized dildo!!"

"But Otis wasted no time," I went on. "He stepped behind Vinny and pressed the tip of the monstrous dildo against Vinny's hole."

"OUCH, his poor hole," Don said.

"Yeah, the poor fucking guy," Robert agreed.

"Let me continue," I said and gulped my beer. "When the dildo was only halfway in Vinny was shaking uncontrollably. He tried to relax to give the dildo easier entry, but that was impossible, seeing as he was in too much pain. Sweat was pouring down his muscular body in what seemed like torrents. He begged them, he pleaded with them, he cried for Cleeve and Otis to stop, but the two men seemed to have Satan himself in them. They mocked Vinny, telling him that his hole was eating up the dildo. Actually, little by little and inch by horrible inch, Vinny's hole WAS eating up that monster dildo. Then, unbelievably, the fifth dildo was in, all the way. Cleeve and Otis stepped back to watch our buddy writhe miserably on the table."

"Shit," Robert said softly. "What the fuck happened then?"

"Vinny passed out," I replied. "When he came to it was midafternoon. He found himself in the back of the van, strapped tightly to the cot, dressed in what was left of his clothes. The van was moving, bringing Vinny home, although he didn't know that at the time. He passed out again, this time in utter exhaustion. The next time he woke up, Vinny found himself sitting in the alley behind this building. He was sitting on the ground next to some garbage pails, dressed in his suit jacket minus his shirt, his suit pants minus his briefs and his shoes and socks.

As he opened his eyes he saw a stray cat licking one of his suede wingtips.

Vinny shooed the cat away and slowly pulled himself to his feet. His nipples, his asshole, and his butt cheeks were all in agony. He walked slowly to the front of the building and rang my doorbell. I let him in and then he sat in this room and sipped scotch, telling me the entire story that I just told you guys. I, like you two could not believe what I was hearing. Vinny looked horribly exhausted and totally beat to shit, both physically and mentally."

"Shit," Robert said. "That was some story Chris."

"I thought you would think so," I said to him. "So be careful out there. Those two guys, Cleeve and Otis were never caught, from what I know that is.

"Did Vinny report it to the police?" Robert asked me.

"No, he felt it would have been too humiliating to report it," I replied.

"When did you last hear from Vinny?" Don asked me.

"About a week or so ago," I said. "He's doing okay so far in California. We don't always talk about that day, but when we do Vinny tells me how he keeps his doors locked all the time and that he never leaves for work till the sun has come up."

"Wow, the poor fucking guy," Robert said. "Do you think he'll ever get over it?"

"Sure, he will," I replied with a small smile. "Vinny is tough and strong, remember?"

"Yeah, I remember," Robert said.

Epilogue

Robert and Don left a short while later. I locked the door and smiled wickedly. I had told my story. My story, God, I loved the sound of that. The only part of it that was not true was the part about Vinny having moved to California. I walked to a small bathroom just past the living room in my condominium apartment, went in and pushed aside the false wall that I had created in there, revealing the small room behind it. Vinny was sitting securely bound to a chair wearing just a pair of knee length (OTC if you prefer) black nylon dress socks. There was a long swatch of duct tape over his mouth, effectively gagging him. He looked up at me beseechingly as I squatted next to him and squeezed one of his nipples good and hard, getting a good moan out of him from behind his gag.

"How're you doing Vinny?" I asked him. "Well, I told Don and Robert all about your ordeal with Cleeve and Otis and I told them that you had moved to California. But then, you already know all that, seeing as you probably heard all of it from in here. I'm sure it was more than frustrating for you listening to me, tell them your story. More frustrating I'll bet was not being able to call out to them for help. No one will look for you here Vinny, *no one.*"

Tears flowed from Vinny's eyes as I stood up, stood behind him and trailed my fingertips over his sideburns. You see, after Vinny had told me his story that day I could not resist the feelings it caused to manifest in me. After Vinny had consumed his third glass of scotch he passed out on my couch. I quickly undressed the well-muscled guy and put him in the secret room I had constructed long ago, for what reason I did not know until that moment.

When Vinny came to he panicked. Since then he's been with me. I cleaned out his apartment and his bank accounts. He has no real family to speak of so no one will look for him. I sent his place of work a letter of resignation, typed from him so that they would not look for him either. And besides, if anyone did look for the hunky Vinny who would ever think of looking for him in my bathroom? I lovingly trailed my fingertips over his sideburns once again, kissed the top of his head and reached down to give one of his nipples another harder squeeze.

Vinny's semi erect cock instantly grew fully hard and engorged. I milk him once every two weeks or so. That keeps Vinny good and hard, good and fucking horny, and his balls in constant pain. One orgasm leaves the poor guy wanting and *needing* more. I keep the muscle boy sedated most of the time, tied up all of the time, and scantily dressed in just his socks, a fresh pair every day. Once in a while I allow him to wear a pair of tight fitting white briefs, but not all that often. I don't want anything rubbing against that great manhood of his, giving him the chance to shoot his load. I kissed Vinny's gagged mouth, left him alone in the room and went back out to the living room to watch some television...

Coming Out the Hard Way

Author: Christopher Trevor

Before I begin my short story of my night with Christopher let me first tell you a little about myself. My name is Mike; I'm thirty-seven years old. I stand about five ten, have brown thinning hair on the sides and I'm bald on top. My eyes are midnight blue and I'm pretty muscular from years of playing ball, lifting weights, and jogging. I work as a corporate manager for a jewelry corporation and I've ALWAYS kept my private life and work separate. I'm gay and I never wanted anyone in my work life to know. I'm far from obvious, being very masculine and all but I think other gay men in the company always suspected me, being that I'm not married and never talk about women or a girlfriend. But I didn't care. Let them suspect all they want. I was there to do a job, not explain my sexual preference. Unfortunately all of that came to an end on a Friday night after work recently.

It had been a very hectic day so I figured I would have a drink before heading home. I went to a bar called Uncle Charlie's South on Third Avenue and Thirty Sixth Street in Manhattan. Its twenty two blocks and six avenues from where I work. No chance of anyone I work with seeing me there, or so I thought. The bar was crowded and there were no seats available. I ordered a beer and stood by the wall, staring at no one in particular. I was dressed in a pair of charcoal colored trousers, white striped shirt, a silk patterned necktie, black slip-on loafers, black ribbed calf-length dress socks, and a black leather jacket. I noticed guys looking at me but I paid no attention to them. I wasn't interested in meeting anyone, at least not in a bar. Then, the door to the bar opened and Christopher walked in. I gulped hard in terror. Christopher works on the same floor where I work at the jewelry company. He's also the most open and out gay man in the entire company. I watched him approach the bar and order a drink.

I was frozen. He was going to see me and then on Monday my secret would no longer be a secret. I could hear them all gloating over the gay muscle head, the jock. If I tried to walk out of the bar I would have to pass right by Christopher. No chance. Christopher got his drink and headed toward the back of the bar. As he was walking he saw me. At first he looked surprised, but then the look on his face turned into what appeared to be triumph as he came over to me.

"Well, well, well," Christopher said. "Mike, of all people and in of all places."

He stood close to me as I took a gulp of my beer. I said hello to him, trying to mask the panic that was evident in my voice, fat chance on that. I was shaking and Christopher knew it.

"I always had a feeling you were gay," Christopher said as he toyed with my necktie.

I explained to him that I was a very private person and practically begged him not to tell anyone at work on Monday. Christopher smiled mockingly and said we had to sit down and talk.

"There are no seats," I said.

"We can sit in the back where it's less crowded and quiet," Christopher replied.

He hooked a finger around one of the belt loops on my trousers and we walked together to the back of the bar where there were long benches set up for seating. We sat down on the top tier.

I crossed one leg on my knee and Christopher placed a hand on my foot, running his hand up and under my pants leg, toying with my sock, taking liberties as it were.

"Want another beer?" he asked me.

"I'm okay for now," I replied. "Thanks."

"I wasn't going to buy it for you," Christopher went on.

I looked at him helplessly, feeling trapped. He continued toying with my sock, playfully snapping the elastic in it, and pulling on the hairs on my leg.

"Now, let's talk," Christopher said.

He explained that he would not tell anyone at work that I was gay as long as I did him a favor. I didn't need three guesses to know what the favor was. He continued by telling me how he was and always had been very attracted to me. He said that he liked the way my tits pressed against my white dress shirts and he had always wanted a taste of them. As he said that I must admit that my cock grew hard as a rock and stalked up in my pants. I love having my tits worked on. As Christopher spoke his lips and mine moved closer and closer to each other's until… we kissed and kissed and kissed. I felt Christopher's hand move to my chest and he squeezed one of my tits under my shirt. When we stopped kissing he said he wanted me to come back to his apartment with him for the night, or else. Fuck and I had just kissed the guy no less. Well, I was in no position to argue or refuse. Part of me felt helpless as we left the bar after another drink each, and another part of me felt elated as I would no doubt have my tits worked on.

We took the train to Christopher's apartment in Brooklyn. I was not given a grand tour of his place. Instead, he brought me directly to the bedroom where a large four poster bed dominated the room. Christopher threw his arms around my big neck and kissed me on the lips. I held him and felt his hands on the back of my neck, this time toying with my shirt collar. He kissed my cheeks, my eyes, and my neck. Both of us were hard and throbbing in our trousers at that point.

"Going to work you hard Mikey boy," Christopher panted in my ear as he hugged me tighter and tighter. "I'm going to do things to you that you've never dreamed of."

Christopher kissed my lips again, followed by my cheeks, eyes and neck. He even licked my neck a few times and then kissed me all over my face again, devouring me, holding me by the back of my neck. Moments later I found myself stripped to my white Calvin Klein briefs and black calf length dress socks. And lo and fucking behold, fucking Christopher had tied me to his four poster bed by my wrists, stretched out on both sides of me, and he had blindfolded me as well.

"Is this your idea of fun?" I asked as I heard Christopher getting undressed.

"Sure is," Christopher replied. "I love seeing a big hunk's ass tied up and helpless."

Christopher climbed onto the bed and sat down in front of me. He began sucking my tits.

"OHHHH yeah," I moaned happily.

As he sucked my right tit he pinched my left one. As he sucked my left tit he pinched my right one. And on and on it went until both my tits were hard and erect. I stretched my legs out on the bed as Christopher moved his tongue down my hairy chest to my stomach, drooling all over me.

"Feels so damned good," I said breathlessly.

I then felt Christopher's tongue moving over the elastic waistband in my briefs. My cock was so hard by now that I thought it would literally burst through the cotton material. I moaned in ecstasy as Christopher tongued my briefs all over, sniffing them at the same time. He then slowly pulled the briefs off me and tongued my balls and the shaft of my big hard cock. I was left wearing just my black dress socks.

"Nice cock Mikey boy, real nice," Christopher teased me. "Bet you'd love for me to suck it for you eh?"

"Oh yes, please," I replied hopefully.

Christopher laughed and said that I would have to wait for that. He resumed tonguing my balls. But then, Christopher snapped a finger against one of my balls, sending a sliver of pain through my body.

"ARRRGHH!!!" I roared in the sudden pain.

He snapped my other ball.

"H-hey!! I wailed. "Are you crazy? Easy with my nuts man!!

Christopher gave each of my balls a few more snaps each and then snapped a cock-ring onto my cock and balls.

"OH God!!" I moaned helplessly. "What the fuck are you going to do to me next?"

Christopher answered my question by stretching my legs apart and tying each of my feet to the posts at the foot of the bed. What a helpless position I was in now. Yet, somehow, I found it all to be oh so exciting. Christopher then began licking the bottoms of my feet, alternately, with the very tip of his tongue, tickling me. I began laughing softly, but as his tongue moved faster over the bottoms and sides of my feet I laughed harder and harder.

"Ticklish aren't you Mikey boy?" Christopher asked.

"Y-yes…YES…" I sputtered. "P-please stop!!"

I thrashed wildly on the bed, helpless against the binding ropes as Christopher's tongue moved all over my socked feet. A few moments later I was sweating and spit was flying out of my mouth as I roared with laughter. Christopher was now holding one of my feet by my toes and running the tip of his finger up and down the bottom of my foot. I begged him to stop. I pleaded with him to let up a little. He simply ignored me and went to work on my other foot. I laughed so hard and mightily that at one point I thought I would piss all over myself. I didn't though.

Finally, Christopher stopped tickling my feet. He moved up close to me and gently kissed me on the lips. I was sweating profusely. Christopher commented that I smelled like a locker room. He kissed my lips again, and again.

Next, I felt Christopher roll a condom onto my hard, erect and throbbing cock. I wanted to cum so badly at this point that my cock felt like it was about to overflow with my sexy jazz. Christopher straddled me, sitting on my crotch area. He told me that he was going to put my cock up his ass for a few minutes but that I was not to cum into the condom. If I did cum he said that he would make me drink my jazz out of the condom. I told Christopher that I would do my best to control myself. He lubed his hole and then slowly slid his asshole down onto my cock.

"OHHHH, nice Mike, your pole in my hole feels so fucking good!" Christopher moaned.

He didn't rock up and down and I didn't thrust him, but God knows I sure as all hell wanted to. Christopher simply sat on my cock, relishing the feel of it in his hole.

He leaned over and caressed the back of my neck, toyed with the knot in my blindfold, kissed my lips a few times and squeezed both my tits at the same time.

"OHHHHHH Christopher," I pleaded. "I want to cum so badly, please..."

"You do that and you know what happens Mike," Christopher stated harshly.

Christopher sat on my cock a while more, then, he climbed off me and said that he was going to leave me alone for a while, adding that he had some things to take care of. I begged him not to leave me tied up this way, but he refused to untie me.

"Then would you at least take the blindfold off me?" I asked hopefully.

That request Christopher fulfilled. He took the blindfold off me and walked naked out of the bedroom, closing the door behind him. So there I was, tied in a spread-eagle position on Christopher's bed, wearing just a pair of my black dress socks. The cock ring tortured my poor hard cock and dangling balls and the condom looked like a sock rolled onto my still stiffening cock. I sweated and squirmed on the bed.

A Half Hour Later...

Christopher came back into the bedroom and sat down next to me on the bed. He asked me if I was enjoying myself. I told him that in a weird sort of way I was. Smiling, he held up my blindfold and said it was time to put it back on me. With that he leaned over me and tied the white cloth back over my eyes, plunging me into darkness once more. One of Christopher's tits was very near my lips so I stuck out my tongue and stole a lick. Christopher pulled his tit away from my mouth and harshly stated, "There will be plenty of time for that later! Right now you're still earning my silence for next week at work!"

Christopher then climbed off the bed. I heard a drawer open and close. He untied my feet and pushed my legs back together until my feet were flat down on the bed with my knees in the air...and my poor asshole a ready target.

"Stick out your tongue!" Christopher commanded. "And make sure it's good and fucking wet! You're going to need a lot of spit!"

I did as I was told and felt a soft plastic object touch my tongue.

"Lick it!" Christopher demanded.

As I licked the object over I realized that it was a dildo. Christopher pushed it into my mouth and forced me to suck on it, drenching it some more.

"Know what it is?" Christopher asked me teasingly.

I nodded. With that Christopher took off my blindfold and held the dildo up in front of me. It was white, really long, and fat. There were two long straps on the end of it. I looked at it in horror.

"Y-you wouldn't," I stammered.

"Oh yes I would," Christopher said as he squeezed one of my tits. "This dildo is going to take a trip up your ass, all the way Mikey boy."

That said, Christopher placed the saliva drenched dildo against my asshole. I clenched my teeth in anticipation and grimaced as I felt the tip of it being pushed into me.

"Christopher please," I begged.

"You have to take it Mikey boy," Christopher stated. "If you don't I'll tell anyone and everyone at work on Monday that you're gay."

All at once I remembered that that was the reason I was there.

I asked Christopher to push the dildo in slowly, a little at a time. I figured that would help me be able to take it. He laughed meanly, giving the dildo a push. Now it was halfway in. I screamed in pain and tears flooded my eyes. When the dildo was more than halfway in I was shaking, sweating, and screaming in agony. Christopher was relentless though, for all at once he rammed the dildo all the way in and crossed the straps on it around my waist and buckled them. The dildo was now tightly fastened into my poor hole and not coming out till Christopher took it out. My screaming had reached a high crescendo so Christopher decided to gag me...with one of his dirty socks. He crammed the foul scented sock into my mouth and tied a rope over it, jamming it firmly in place.

"I'll bet that tastes yummy huh Mikey boy?" Christopher asked mockingly.

I writhed in agony as Christopher stretched my legs back and retied them by my ankles to the bedposts. Smiling, Christopher leaned over my right foot and sucked my sock covered toes. My cock was harder than it had been earlier and pressing against the condom still rolled over it. I could see the pre cum all over the tip of it as Christopher sucked my toes, sending chills through me. I was in pain and ecstasy at the same damned time. Christopher then looked into my eyes and smiled. Saliva dripped from the sides of my gagged mouth as I shook in pain and ecstasy.

"Want to cum really badly now huh?" Christopher asked, pointing at my erection.

I nodded with pleading showing in my eyes.

"Not yet Mikey boy," Christopher replied mockingly.

That said, Christopher stood up, walked out of the room, and closed the door behind him, leaving me alone again.

Christopher returned within ten minutes this time. His cock was hard and swinging freely between his legs. He said it was time for me to suck his cock. As soon as he shot his load I was to swallow every drop of him, then, and only then would he take the dildo out of my ass, the cock ring off my cock, and he would allow me to cum into the condom. For his complete silence at work on Monday I would have to guzzle down my cum from out of the condom. I nodded in agreement to all of my captor's terms, and as I nodded Christopher took his mangy sock out of my mouth. I then verbally agreed to all his demands, not to mention that I was horny as a cat in heat at that moment.

Moments later I was kneeling on the floor in front of Christopher. My hands were roped behind me and my feet were securely tied together as well, Christopher sat on the bed and gently caressed the back of my neck as I sucked his hard cock. His cock tasted delicious, to say the least. I just had to admit to that. He forced his cock deep into my throat a few times, made me lick his balls, and then suck him some more. About five minutes later Christopher shot his load.

"OH YEAH, yeah," he moaned loudly as he stuck to his word and forced me to swallow every drop of his cum.

And what a load it was that he forced me to scoff down. Fuck, it seemed to go on and on. I swallowed it hungrily and greedily. When Christopher was done he let his cock slip out of my mouth. I looked up at him hopefully. I mean, my cock was past the boiling point. It was screaming and aching to cum, and still trapped in the condom. And my balls, my God, my balls felt like they were filled with gallons of my spunk.

"Ready Mikey boy?" Christopher asked.

"Ready," I replied happily.

Christopher untied my feet and ordered me to stand up. Once again I did as I was told. He leaned me against a wall, grabbed my erection and began jacking me the fuck off. And as he jacked me harder and harder he took one of my tits into his mouth.

"OH YEAH, fuck yeah," I roared.

I squirmed around as the dildo still tortured my hole, but what Christopher was doing overpowered the pain. As Christopher sucked my tit and jacked me off I shot my load…and shot my load…and fucking shot my load…into the condom.

"OHHHHH FUUUCCCKKK YEAH!!" I screamed and arched my back as my cum filled up the condom. "OHHHH YESSSS…"

When I was done spewing my load the dildo in my ass suddenly tortured me all the more. It seemed that after shooting my load every part of me became more sensitive to the touch, especially my dildo filled asshole. I begged Christopher to take the gizmo out of my hole, but he said that I had one more promise to fulfill. With that he slowly peeled the condom off my cock.

I opened my mouth and he poured my own cum into it. I swallowed it all. Fuck, I had eaten my own cum and I was totally turned on all over again because of it.

Christopher gave each of my tits a playful tug and said, "Good boy Mikey, you did very well indeed."

"And, and you won't tell anyone at work on Monday that I'm gay?" I asked him.

"I always keep my word," Christopher replied.

Then, Christopher undid the straps on the dildo and yanked it out of my hole. It came out followed by a fart. We both laughed. Finally, Christopher took the cock ring off my cock and balls and untied my hands. We looked at each other, smiled and hugged. Christopher's mouth found mine and we kissed long, hungrily and passionately.

"Would you like to stay the night with me Mike?" Christopher asked.

"Do I have a choice this time?" I asked him.

Christopher smiled, gave my tits a squeeze each, and said, "Of course you have a choice Mike. I would never have said anything on Monday, even if you hadn't come back here with me tonight. If you don't want anyone at work knowing that you're gay that's your prerogative. I just used it as a way to get you tied up and have some fun with you."

A wave of relief swept me up in its arms. Christopher was a gentleman after all, or at least he seemed to be, ha, ha fucking ha.

I then told him that I would stay the night with him. That said, Christopher grinned meanly and retied my hands behind me and blindfolded me again.

About the Author

Christopher Trevor

Christopher Trevor was born in July 1963 and grew up in New York City. As soon as he was old enough to know how he began writing fiction and has been writing gay erotic/fetish stories for the past ten to twelve years at this point. He became an avid reader as well from the time he knew how and reads everything from fiction, to non-fiction to biographies of interesting and unusual people, people who have made a difference  or who have paved the way for others. Christopher attributes his writing artistic inspiration to artists such as Etienne, Tom of Finland, Tagame, The Hun, and most notably Joe T, who Christopher has had the pleasure of speaking with and even meeting over the last few years. Christopher states, "Joe T encouraged me to write about my fetish because I was embarrassed about it at the time. Joe T said that when we are embarrassed about something that makes it even more enticing somehow." Christopher totally agreed and never stopped writing in this genre. Erotic writers who inspired Christopher Trevor were: Tom Shaw (author of "That Day at the Quarry), C.S. White (author of Big Sur), Larry Townsend (author of countless erotic novels), and Mason Powell (author of the classic story "The Brig.")

Christopher discovered that not only did he enjoy writing erotic tales but that after his first bondage experience he had a genuine flair for it. Writing to erotic oriented magazines about his first bondage experience truly opened the floodgates for Christopher where this style of writing is concerned. Christopher thanks the handsome and muscular "Greg" for that experience way back in time. Christopher took "Creative Writing" courses every semester during his high school years and while other friends of his stopped writing what they loved to write about as time went on Christopher never let a day go by when he didn't write something... "I feel that if I don't write every day I will die," Christopher has said many times over.

Foot fetish stories and all things related; spanking fetish, erotic shaving, muscle bondage, tickle torture, and hardcore stories are just a few of the areas of gay eroticism that Christopher enjoys writing about and inspiring in others as well. As one internet buddy said to Christopher where the black socks fetish is concerned, "Until I started talking with you I never gave a thought to my socks when I got dressed for work in the morning. Now when I pull my dress socks on every morning I get a chill up my spine."

Christopher is proud of the erotic effect he has on people...

Christopher Trevor is also the author of:

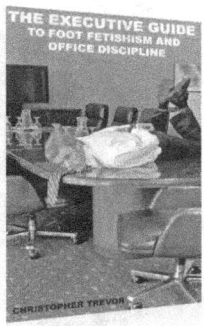

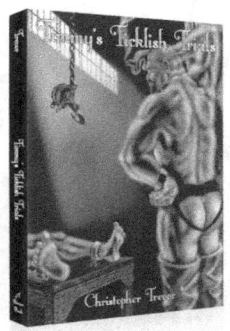

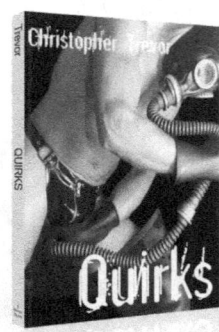

HUMILIATION — Christopher Trevor

a tribute to Leather — Edited and Compiled by Christopher Trevor

DISCIPLINE — COMPILED BY Christopher Trevor

CLEEVE AND OTIS STRIKE AGAIN — CHRISTOPHER TREVOR

REVENGE — CHRISTOPHER TREVOR

MEN AT WORK — CHRISTOPHER TREVOR

Quirks II — Christopher Trevor

OBSESSIONS — Edited by Christopher Trevor

MEN AT WORK II — CHRISTOPHER TREVOR

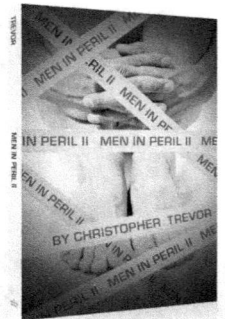

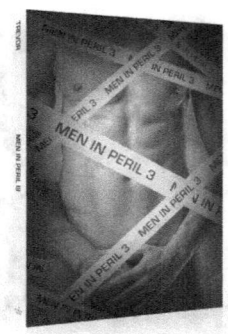

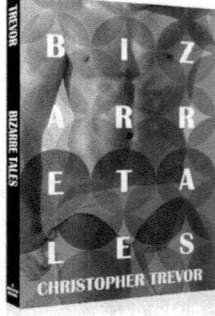